He looked down and her eyes met his.

"There's no time to hesitate."

She pulled her hand free.

"Who are you?"

"No time. I'm here to get you out."

"How do I know that?"

"Look," he gritted out. "There's no time to offer proof. You have two choices. Trust me or..." He nodded his head backward, where it was obvious only death waited.

She stood there almost rocking on her heels. He could see the indecision, the unwillingness to trust any further, and he didn't blame her.

"I'm saying this only once more before I throw you over my shoulder. We can do it your way or we can do it mine."

SUSPECT WITNESS

RYSHIA KENNIE

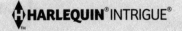

For Ken—who led the journey through Malaysia's Gunung Mulu
caves with the feeble light of a travel flashlight.
Our hiking boots were ankle-deep in bat guano and each step
was treacherous. I clutched the back of his shirt
as I couldn't always see in the fleeting light.
But the vast beauty of the cave was worth a ton of bat guano.

ISBN-13: 978-0-373-69889-9

Suspect Witness

Copyright © 2016 by Patricia Detta

PLEASE RECYCLE
THIS PRODUCT IS RECYCLABLE

Recycling programs
for this product may
not exist in your area.

Printed in U.S.A.

™ www.Harlequin.com

Ryshia Kennie has received a writing award from the City of Regina, Saskatchewan, and also been a semifinalist in the Kindle Book Awards. She finds that there's never a lack of places to set an edge-of-the-seat suspense, as prairie winters find her dreaming of warmer places for heart-stopping stories. They are places where deadly villains threaten intrepid heroes and heroines who battle for their right to live or even to love. For more, visit ryshiakennie.com.

Books by Ryshia Kennie

Harlequin Intrigue

Suspect Witness

CAST OF CHARACTERS

Josh Sedovich—A CIA field agent, his latest assignment is to locate a woman who fled the scene of a murder. But things get complicated when he not only locates her, but he finds himself falling for the woman he's sworn to protect.

Erin Kelley Argon—A suspected witness to murder, this primary school teacher is now being targeted by the Anarchists, a dangerous gang. To protect everything she holds dear, she changes her identity, flees her home and runs halfway across the globe.

Mike Olesk—A retired San Diego city police officer and an old family friend. He's determined to help Erin, but his skills are rusty and his advice may have steered her wrong.

Antonio Enrique—The murdered Spanish billionaire may have funded some of the Anarchists' illicit activities. But none of that is proven before he's killed, with Erin as a witness.

Steven Decker—He dated Erin until she discovered who he really was. As a member of the Anarchists biker gang, he thinks he knows Erin's secret, for he was there on the day that Antonio Enrique was murdered.

Sarah Argon—Pregnant, single and with no career aspirations, Erin's younger sister has always depended on Erin to protect her.

Wade Gair—A pilot with a late start in a CIA career. He's flown Josh out of numerous trouble spots. Struggling under the financial burden of alimony, he dreams about financial freedom.

Derrick Reese—The head of the outlaw biker gang the Anarchists. He'll do anything to stop the witness and keep both his gang's deadly secret and himself from facing justice.

Tenuk Laksana—A Malaysian Special Forces agent, he's been assigned to assist in securing the Gulung Mulu Park area. Despite his diminutive size, he'll hold up his end as long as Josh needs him and he'll kill anyone who gets in his way.

Vern Ferguson—The director of Josh's branch of the CIA. It is through him that Josh is able to make what contact he can with the home office.

Chapter One

Singapore—Saturday, October 10

She had been pretty once.

Now her skin gleamed in the glow of the fluorescent lights. A strand of auburn hair fell across a well-shaped brow and her lips held a glimmering trace of sherbet lip gloss.

"It's a shame, really," the coroner said as his sun-bronzed hand held the edge of the stark white sheet. "Life was just getting started. Twenty-five or there about." He shook his head. "I try to remember that every time I step out of the house. Enjoy the moment. You just never know. And in this job you're reminded of mortality every day." A strand of salt-and-pepper hair drifted across his forehead. "I try not to think about it or it would drive me crazy."

"True," Josh Sedovich said. "Any idea how she died?"

The coroner nodded. "She was hit by a blunt object to the back of the head. Surprising, I always thought Singapore so civilized until I moved here and took this job. Unfortunately, it's turned out no better than anywhere else."

"Why does it always end like this? On a temporary visa to see the world and, just like that, it's over." Josh ran his hand along the side of his neck. "It's damn hot in here."

"No air-conditioning," the coroner said. "Is she who you're looking for?"

"No. Fortunately not." He fisted his right hand. Not so fortunately for the unknown young woman on the coroner's slab.

Probable murder, potential arson and an unknown assassin. He'd been on the trail of this case for the past three weeks, and now one person was dead and still, miraculously, the witness lived. Not only lived but thrived over days that had turned into weeks and weeks into months. It wouldn't have happened had the FBI called him in sooner.

"Interesting that Victor has given you a hall pass. Maybe the fact that she's American, too. But more than likely not." The coroner looked at Josh with mild interest. "Private investigator..." He frowned. "I thought you would have to be a little more than that. CIA maybe. Or maybe I just watch too much television."

Josh slipped his hand into his pocket and looked away before meeting the coroner's gaze. "American? How do you know that?"

"Assumption on my part, but look at this." He pulled down the sheet, exposing the cadaver's torso, and pointed at her belly button. A steel stud pierced her navel; the steel was offset only by the red, white and blue of the American flag.

"Maybe," Josh said doubtfully. "But she might be a wannabe, too."

"Yeah, I know. Or her boyfriend was or, or... Still comes down to an unidentified body."

He straightened, turning to face Josh. "'Course, tattoos, earrings..." He trailed off, looking pointedly at the metal ace of spades in Josh's left ear. "Are rather a dime a dozen." He shook his head. "Don't understand it much. Must be the generation gap." An overhead fan kicked on. "What's this girl done? Any ideas on why someone murdered her?"

"Nothing that I know of." Josh flexed his fingers as he looked at the sad, lifeless figure. He reached over and took the corner of the sheet and pulled it up over her breasts. "Wrong place. Wrong time."

"Seems a little more than wrong place and time. Someone torched her apartment, but not before killing her." The coroner coughed into his gloved hand. "Heard that the original lease is in a different name, sublet. Can't get hold of the girl who signed the lease to tell us who she sublet to. Traveling Europe or some such idiocy."

"Just a minute." Josh held up his forefinger before turning his back and taking a few steps away. He pulled out the cell phone he'd bought at a local convenience store and hit Redial. "Yeah, Victor. I'll be there in a half hour, maybe less." He slipped the phone back into his pocket.

"Well, I suppose we'll know who she is soon enough." The coroner slid the drawer containing the body back into place and out of sight.

Twenty minutes later, Josh stepped over the charred threshold of the ruined apartment building. Outside, the cinder brick exterior was still intact but inside was a gutted mess. Water dripped from the ceiling and the acrid smell of burned plastic mixed with wood smoke and other synthetics.

He covered his mouth with the back of his hand and coughed.

"Josh Sedovich." Victor Chong held out his hand. It was a quick shake, more a formality than one with any feeling.

"Chong." He shook the man's hand for the second time that day. "Still can't convince you that a private investigator might get you more information than this team of officials you're set on?"

"No more than you could this morning."

"Definitely a case of arson," Victor confirmed with a shake of his head. His safety helmet was tucked under his arm and there were smudges of soot across his cheek. His dark hair was matted to his head and it was obvious that he had spent a great deal of time inside the smoking and charred remains. "Have you seen the body?"

"I did."

"And?" Victor arched a brow. "Was she the girl you're looking for? Your lost person?"

"No idea who she might be, but she isn't who I'm looking for." He glanced beyond Victor into the small studio apartment where she'd lived.

"Can't imagine hunting missing persons day in and day out. No variety."

"It's a job like any other," he said shortly.

"Now if that wasn't a false statement," Victor replied. "People go missing for all sorts of reasons, and I'll bet you've seen them all. So, best-case scenario that she's not in the morgue yet. I mean the one you're looking for. Obviously, the other… Well, we both know where she is."

"Best-case scenario, it wasn't her," Josh agreed, turning to look at the damage the fire had done. "Too bad about the identification bit. You would have made my job easier."

Victor shrugged. "Although identification isn't my problem, I still wouldn't mind having one up on Detective Tay. He's a prideful bugger, always rubbing my nose in it."

Josh stepped around Victor, his gaze taking in the cheaply papered walls, the hint of a vine pattern only partially concealed by soot and smoke. The tiny apartment was pretty much ruined. The water had destroyed what the fire hadn't.

"Interesting that the body wasn't burned at all. Now

it's just a matter of getting the right people to view her. And then we'll get that damn ID."

Josh breathed lightly as he stepped into the room. Victor carried on his one-way conversation as he followed. The smell of smoke was more intense here as it saturated the air and bit harshly into his sinuses. His stomach rolled. He looked with envy at the mask Victor donned as he stepped over a pool of water and sodden books that were scattered around a fallen bookcase.

The dull red spine of a hard cover copy of *Wuthering Heights* lay across the top of a box of paperbacks whose bright and torrid covers curled and swelled. The classic was like an old dog in the midst of a pack of pups. He skirted a small, nondescript, collapsed wooden table— more cardboard than wood, the kind purchased in discount box stores—and walked over to a small desk that stood untouched except for the damp soot that clung to it. The desk was different from the other furniture in the room. It looked older and had character. The patina was richer and darker, the legs had deep scrolls carved into them that swirled through the wood. He slipped on a glove and opened a side drawer. There was nothing but a collection of elastic bands, tape, pens and blank notepads. The heat had not gotten to this part of the room. He did a quick take of the other side drawer. This time it opened to a small line of files. His fingers flitted quickly through them, stopped and went back. From the corner of his eye he saw Victor watching. He wasn't sure how long Victor would allow his surreptitious view of the apartment before demanding that the fire investigative team and police take over. It was a lull in the investigation. The fire had only been out a few hours, and Josh was taking full advantage as he had done in other crime scenes in other countries throughout the world. It was all about speed and timing. He left the files and moved to the middle drawer.

He took out a blue leather folder and pushed the metal release. The folder opened; nothing was inside. He glanced over his shoulder. Victor was not looking. His attention went to the bottom side drawer, and his fingers skimmed quickly through the files.

He flipped through papers in a cardboard file. Empty—except one small sheet and a receipt. Both bore the name Erin and one Erin Kelley.

Tell Mike I took his last advice.

The note was written in a careful script, the letters fine, unlike a more masculine scroll that only confirmed what the signature said. The writer was Erin Kelley, or at least the woman currently calling herself that. The woman who had so recently been Erin Kelley Argon before she'd changed her passport and her last name. A twist of fate twenty-nine years ago had her parents on a business trip in Canada where her mother went into early labor. As a result, Erin qualified for citizenship in that country and when she'd run, she'd taken advantage of it. He took both pieces of evidence, folded them one-handed and slipped them into his pocket. He closed the drawer and opened the middle drawer and retraced the fine line he'd felt earlier. He pushed and something gave. He pulled open the drawer farther to reveal a hidden compartment.

"What do you have?" Victor was beside him. "The authorities only did a cursory look before they took the body away. And I just got here. So anything you can do to make our job easier." He pulled the thin edge of his moustache with a troubled look. "Although, really, I shouldn't be letting you do this."

Josh ignored the man as he took out an American driver's license and a passport. He flipped open the passport and it only confirmed what the first piece of ID had already told him. "Here's your identification. Emma Whyte. She had it well hidden against thieves."

"By jove. Good work, old chap."

Josh grimaced and rubbed the back of his neck. "Since when did you become a Brit, Vic?"

Victor scowled and glanced at his watch.

"What time is it?"

"Seven o'clock."

"It's been a long day. I'll leave you to it," Josh said. "She's obviously not the woman I was looking for."

"Good luck!" Victor told him genially.

Josh stepped over the threshold, seemingly empty-handed. Once outside, he dialed the number that would be in service for only a few more hours.

"It's not her," he said. "But she was here. Whoever the bastard is that they have on her tail, he now knows her last location."

"What's the matter? You sound off."

"Could be the last two years have been pretty much on the road."

"What, you're telling me you don't love it?"

"Not that much. After this, Vern, I need a vacation. I need to go home."

"To the RV? Josh you're not a family man and you live in a trailer."

His hand went into his pocket, his thumb smoothing the worn bead of a dime-store earring. "It's home, Vern. And family or not, it's time for me to take a break."

"Okay, fine."

He dropped the earring back into his pocket as a door slammed across the street. He walked away from the apartment building and around the corner to where an alley gave him a discreet view of the comings and goings around the apartment. "What gives with this case, Vern? There's another body. A woman. Every bloody assignment… I'm so damned sick of seeing women dead. At least this time she wasn't raped. Not that that is any better. Dead is dead."

"You're taking it personally," Vern Ferguson, the director of Josh's branch in the CIA said.

He turned away from the street and looked down the tight, concrete-bordered alley. Sometimes it was hard not to take it personally. He drew in a breath, held it a few seconds longer than necessary. "You said you have something new? What is it, Vern?" His gaze roamed the area—the overflowing garbage bin, the tiger-striped dog snuffling through the refuse. "I don't think there's much time. We could be talking hours, minutes… Who knows?"

"Intelligence has her in Georgetown, Malaysia."

"Georgetown. Damn it, Vern. Too bad you didn't have that for me sooner. You know the Anarchists don't waste time. They're not just any biker gang. As it is she's been running for five months."

"Yeah, I know," Vern said with a hitch in his voice that was part wheeze, part cough. "She's tired and with the trial going forward, they won't stop."

"Right, and they want her dead, and odds are they're on their way. Fortunately, no one knows where in Georgetown yet."

"Then quit wasting time on the damn phone."

Josh grimaced as he clicked off and tossed the phone into a nearby garbage can.

Chapter Two

"Give Respect, Get Respect." Erin Kelley repeated the words as she wrote the phrase on the chalkboard and ended with a sweeping flourish. Her fingers shook and she had to stop. She ran her tongue along her lower lip, her back to the class. But even writing the word *respect* sent a slight tremor through her. The chalk dust clung uncomfortably to her sweaty palm.

The temperature was unseasonably warm and this early in the morning the heat was already unbearable in the small, cramped room. A finger of light skittered across the blackboard, briefly illuminating the words. She mentally shrank from the light as if under a searchlight, as if they'd found her after all these months. Impossible, she reminded herself as the chalk sweated in her hand, and the children shifted anxiously behind her. And as she had done so many times before, she reminded herself that she was safe, that her trail was cold. Enough time had elapsed. They'd never find her. They were no longer interested. And as she did at odd times throughout any given day, she considered the truth of those beliefs and whether she was really safe, whether these children were safe. One day, she knew, despite her hopes, the answer would have her on the run again but that wasn't today.

She put down the chalk and turned to face the class.

"Today, we're going to learn about respect," she said in English. The school's curriculum was taught in English to children who were already bilingual, fluent in both Malay and English, and who, in many cases, if they hadn't already, would master a third or even fourth language in their lifetime.

At the back of the room a heavyset boy shifted in his seat. Beside him, a sullen-faced classmate shuffled papers across his desk. And at the front one boy whispered furtively to another. The rest of the boys eyed her uneasily. They knew what was coming. There wasn't a boy who had missed the taunting in the schoolyard and not one who didn't know what was going to happen as a result. She had made it all perfectly clear from her first day.

She fixed her gaze on the targets of this lecture. The two culprits dressed in crisply pressed navy pants with matching jackets, white shirts and sleek haircuts stared back without a flicker of emotion. They were both the sons of successful Malaysian businessmen, and neither lacked for pride or esteem. They were children of wealth and privilege with attitudes she had struggled to control since her arrival. Yesterday, their attitudes had threatened to harm another student. It was a scenario that played out in schoolyards across the globe and through the decades. They had taunted a slight, studious boy on the playground. She bit back the scathing words she wanted to say. Bullying aside, they were still only children. But for a second she saw another classroom a world away, and another child and a small girl pummeling another.

Leave my sister alone!

The skinny, carrot-haired girl stuck in her mind, running through reel after reel. The knobby knees, the brilliant hair, the circle of taunting children. And always she stood screaming those words, running intervention as she grabbed and punched and pulled hair, freeing her sister from the circle of tormentors—over and over again.

Her gaze went to the thin boy in the front of the class. He wasn't looking at her. Instead, he was fumbling through his backpack, which was emblazoned with a variety of action figures.

"Before we begin today's lesson, who would like to volunteer to go tell Mr. Daniel that the air conditioner isn't working?"

"They've shut it off, Miss," Ian said. "They always do in October."

"Besides, Mr. Daniel's left." Isaac waved his hand frantically in the air even as he spoke.

"On an errand," Ian added.

"In your new car," Isaac finished. He was fascinated by vehicles of any sort and had followed her into school last week pestering her with details of her new vehicle purchase and clearly unimpressed with what had impressed her; gas mileage.

"Right. I didn't realize he was leaving this soon." She pulled at the back of her cotton blouse, which was beginning to stick. She wiped the back of her hand across her damp brow as her eyes drifted to the parking lot and she thought of Daniel. Friend or not, she wasn't apt to lend out her vehicle on a whim, but Daniel hadn't asked. Instead, he'd planned to use public transport and lose over a half a day's pay to attend a dental appointment. Knowing the pain the tooth was causing him and that he was too proud to ask for help, she'd offered him her car. Insisted, really.

"So, let's begin." She swept a hand to the blackboard. "Respect."

The class of ten- and eleven-year-old boys in their fourth year of the six-year Malaysian primary school system should have been sweating and fidgeting. Instead, they now sat with backs straight, their eyes fixed on her.

"Anyone know what that means?" She placed her hands on the back of her chair. The sunlight seemed to shift and for a moment blinded her. She pushed the small crystal bowl to the front of her desk. The orchid and the bowl were a birthday gift from a group of teachers she'd had lunch with since she'd arrived. They'd presented the gift yesterday and even had sung a round of "Happy Birthday." Except that her birthday wasn't yesterday, nor was it this month. Her birthday was months past and a lifetime away.

"He's a loser." A boy stood up. His height and classic good looks belied his age.

The boy in question sat slouched over his desk, his untidy mop of black hair hanging forward and hiding his face from the class. She looked away and instead forced her gaze to the boy who had just spoken.

"Sit!" she snapped at Jefri. The boy was one of a small, tight-knit group who thought his family's wealth placed him a tier above everyone else. "No one's a loser."

Out of the corner of her eye she saw a flicker of motion. Something moved in the parking lot. She allowed her attention to divert momentarily. Her heart thumped.

"Miss Kelley?" Jefri's voice was insistent and still had the high notes of childhood, despite the fact that at almost twelve, he stood tall enough to face her eye to eye.

"Just a minute." She motioned the boy to sit down. Outside the heat rose in shimmering waves from the pavement as the shadow cast by the voluptuous canopy of an ancient rain tree fell short of cooling the overheated tar. In the parking lot, her new lemon-yellow Naza Sutera gleamed. Daniel hadn't left yet.

Her hand curled on her desk, her nails biting into her palm. A familiar figure moved with an easy walk toward her car, and whatever or whoever had caught her attention previously was gone. She breathed out a sigh as she recognized the school custodian, Daniel.

She turned her attention back to the class as she pointed to the chalkboard. "Shall we read this together?"

"Give Respect. Get Respect," the boys repeated, their childish voices rising solemnly to the occasion, some looking rather sullen, while others repeated dutifully as they did everything she asked.

"So, now we'll discuss what that means. I want—"

A blast of light exploded outside with a roar that rattled the windows and knocked the remainder of her sentence into eternity, where it would remain forgotten. Somewhere outside the room someone screamed.

A door slammed.

"Stay where you are. Sit down, all of you. Now!"

She rushed to the window even as the children jumped from their seats.

Flames shot into the air, smoke billowed, obscuring the parking lot, the grass. "Oh, my God!" She took a stumbling step backward. Her body seemed to freeze in position.

"Miss Kelley?" a small voice questioned her.

"Did you see that?" someone else shouted.

The class, she'd almost forgotten… A boy pushed in beside her, fighting for window space.

Voices chattered in the hallway.

She needed to secure the room. Protect the children.

"Sit!" she repeated as she swung around. "Stay away from the door!" She grabbed the edge of the desk and yanked it in that direction. But already the door had flung open and children scattered into the hallway.

"They're here," she whispered.

Chapter Three

Flames shot in the air as Josh closed the space between him and the fireball that had once been a vehicle. Black smoke billowed through the flames, and the smell of gas and burning metal filled the parking lot. And there was a hint of something else, the putrid sweet scent of burning flesh.

No.

He shielded his eyes from the intense glare and grimaced at the sight of the blackened hulk behind the wheel. He watched silently, aware of two things in that instant—that the corpse was too big to be her and that the outlaw biker gang, the Anarchists, had found her. He backed up and returned to the shelter of a canopy of pepper vines that fronted the edge of the school and provided a leafy shelter. He had no qualms about moving out of sight now that he knew the victim was beyond his help. His attention settled briefly on the burning vehicle. Chaos erupted from the building as children yelled and shrieked. The sharp commands of authority cut through the mass of voices as two female teachers attempted to control a mob of children. He hovered at the corner of the building, away from the main crush, out of sight of curious eyes.

He edged forward. The children milled excitedly, some cupping their hands over their eyes to get a better view.

An older, gray-haired woman in a suit jacket and skirt was hurling orders and pointing inside. When one boy headed for the steps, she yanked him back by the collar of his navy blue school uniform. Josh's gaze went to the other exit.

"Where are you?" He pushed the knit cap back from his forehead and glanced at the car and the fire that continued to burn bright and hot. He turned his attention back to the school and debated rounding the building and entering through the back. But that would serve no purpose. He was well aware that a face-to-face encounter, especially now, would have her running. He'd come too far to lose her.

"Come on," he encouraged his absent quarry. He wondered how she'd managed to survive as long as she had. From what he could see she had only a rudimentary knowledge of the art of disappearing and a bucket of pure luck. That was about to change.

"Daniel!"

It was a woman's voice, clear with a sweet edge despite the shock that so obviously laced through the words.

"There you are," he said under his breath. She had changed her name, her nationality and her look, but he would know her anywhere. Her hair was now a pallid blond contained in an elegant updo that he recognized as an attempt to add years to her youthful face. But even at a distance he would recognize those eyes and those cheekbones. He'd studied that face for hours, memorized it as he did for every job. Except this time he had wanted to know so many other things, such as what her voice sounded like. Now he knew.

Her gaze seemed to fix on the scene. He inched closer.

A movement out of the corner of his eye had him turning, and as he did he saw that one of the children had broken from the cluster and was moving much too close to the vehicle.

"Damn it," he swore. The flames were licking at the vehicle and there was no way of knowing if the gas tank had gone with the first explosion. He moved fast, forgetting about keeping to the fringes or keeping his head low. He grabbed the child and rolled with him, sideways and away from the hot, still-popping metal.

The boy squirmed, and Josh pinned the youngster with one hand. "It might explode again. Stay back unless you want to die." He repeated the command in Malay for good measure.

The boy nodded. Josh let the boy up and watched as he rushed back to his friends, who were all huddled a safe distance away. There was a look of hero worship in the group as the boys gathered around him. The boy was obviously considered a hero for undertaking such a risky business as getting close to the car or possibly being tackled by a strange man, or maybe a combination of the two. The adults were moving out of synch. One woman corralled another group of boys while another was frantically talking on her cell. Near the entrance of the school he could see two others, but all of their attention was focused on the vehicle, and all of them seemed to be moving in a disjointed fashion or not at all.

Josh diverted his attention back to the vehicle. The smoke curled thick and black, and in the distance he could hear the wailing sirens. The canopy of a lone rain tree threw shadows over the shrinking fire in the parking lot, its arthritic trunk standing thick and knotted, a silent silhouette. Across the street a woman clutched the handles of her pedal-powered pushcart, the vibrant pink, yellow and red flowers muted in the gathering smoke. On the main street cars continued to move in a steady stream as if smoke and fire were a normal part of their daily commute.

He scowled. He'd been so close. It had been gut instinct to check the primary schools in Georgetown, suspecting she would hunker down, consider herself safe again for a time. On Sunday, with the help of a local investigator that he'd met on a previous assignment, he'd acquired access to and checked the records of every school in the city that taught in English and that had acquired a foreign female teacher in the past few months.

He'd gone to her apartment just as school would be beginning for the day. While he was fairly certain that they'd located her, he'd hoped to find something that might prove that the woman they'd found in school records was her. He'd jimmied the building's back door. Fortunately the building was old and unalarmed, but who he suspected was the building's owner had found him just as he left her apartment. In fact, he had just closed and locked the door, leaving it as he had found it including the small piece of tissue tucked in the latch, meant to alert her to an intruder. It had taken a bit of acting to back out of that situation, but he'd had what he wanted—confirmation that she was the teacher he was seeking and—what he'd thought at the time was an interesting tidbit of information—that she was the owner of a new Naza Sutera.

In the distance, the Penang hills cast a sinister shadow as they cradled one against the other, their dark protrusions muted by distance. His gaze cruised across the bystanders, did a mental calculation of faces, numbers, positions. Nothing.

Josh gritted his teeth over the expletive that wouldn't change the reality.

She was gone.

Chapter Four

Erin was fighting for breath as she rounded the corner and stood out of sight of the school. A lorry swished past belching exhaust as a convoy of motorcyclists followed close behind. It seemed as though they were all fighting for space as a truck jammed in behind the cyclists and the loud red of Coca-Cola overlaid it all as a delivery truck squeezed into the street. A horn honked and a bicyclist swerved as pedestrians weaved their way through the intersection's traffic snarl.

Her jaw was clenched so tight it ached, and her hand worried the strap of the bag as her eyes strained for a cab to flag. One broke with the traffic and pulled to the curb. She rushed to meet it, throwing open the door and flinging herself inside.

"Focus," she muttered. She fired off her address in panicked words that she had to repeat when the driver turned around with a puzzled look.

Behind her, flames still punctured the otherwise quiet late-morning sky as sirens wailed and trouble inched closer.

"Daniel," she whispered. She dashed a tear away and unclenched her hands. She looked out the window as sun glared through the windscreen. A motorcycle pulled up beside the cab, a chopper. The driver's legs were propped up as he sat back on the low-slung seat. He turned, a dusty-brown beard covering much of his swarthy face, and smiled. The smile was not one of friendship. It was a leer, maybe, or worse. She hit the door lock.

She swallowed and clenched her free hand so tight that her nails dug into her palm. Her throat closed and her eyes burned with unshed tears.

She'd hated to run but she didn't have a choice. The conversation with Mike Olesk had made that fact clear. A retired police officer who had been a friend of her father's and a man she hadn't seen in years, Mike had been the only person she could think of whom she could trust and who might help her sort out her options. The conversation that ensued was one she would never forget, for it had changed her life.

He tapped ashes into a glass ashtray, the Hollywood emblem once sharply emblazoned on it now blurred with ashes. "I know how these things go down. The authorities make promises. But face it, on this one we're talking local police up against the Anarchists. They don't stand a chance. If it were the feds it would be a different matter."

"Why isn't it?" Her stomach turned over, anticipating what he would say.

"It will be soon. The local authorities will be calling you in for questioning, unless you come forward first. I suspect you maybe have a day, maybe less."

"No," she said shortly. "I can't. I won't answer their questions."

"You know you don't have a choice. Why are you balking at this, Erin?"

She shook her head.

"It would be for the best. They could charge you with obstruction of justice."

"I'd go to jail?" There'd be safety in jail.

"Maybe, maybe not." He coughed, the sound deep and achy in the silence between them. "Word's out that the Anarchists will do anything to ensure their leader, Derrick Reese, doesn't serve time. Maybe if I put in a word with the sheriff's office we could have this thing escalated to a federal level. We could live with that."

"I can't."

He rubbed the bridge of his nose with his thumb. "If we don't do that, if you run, that only makes you guilty of a crime."

"I can't. I'll run. Can you help me?"

"Erin. Are you out of your mind? Did you hear what I just told you? If I can get to the feds, if you admit everything, they can keep you safe."

"They'll want me to testify," she repeated, her heart thumping.

"Of course."

"Under oath?"

"Under oath," he agreed. "Erin, what is this all about? Who are you protecting?"

Silence hung between them.

"Who was it, Mike? Who turned me in?"

He took a long drag on a hand-rolled cigarette, his thick brows drawing down over narrow eyes.

"Word has it that only this morning that no-good boyfriend of yours squealed louder than a pig facing a luau."

"Steven," she whispered. And despite everything, the betrayal still hurt. She couldn't trust anyone, not with the truth, not with who was really the witness.

Smoke curled around them and her nose tickled. She wanted to sneeze but instead she coughed.

"Mike, I can't give you details. Just trust me. I have to run. I need to disappear."

"Erin?"

"Mike. Please, can you help me? It's life or death. Please, just trust me."

He stood there looking at her for a long time before he nodded. "For how long?"

"I don't know," she said quietly. "As long as it takes."

"Come." He motioned with one hand. She followed him and together they worked out a plan.

She shuddered. She ached to go home, to where it all began—San Diego. And she knew she might never go home again.

She opened her eyes and for a moment she froze, thoughts of home driven from her mind.

"The children," she murmured. She would have stayed for them, if it had been necessary. But the children were safe. She'd made sure of that. The principal had corralled many of them before they'd exited the building. The ones who had managed to slip outside were under the watchful eyes of two senior teachers.

She'd miss them, even the troublesome ones. Her life had become one of loss, of regret—it was what she hadn't expected of a life on the run, or more aptly what she hadn't thought of until the reality hit.

Focus, she reminded herself as the cab swung onto the congested street that she called home. Overhead, signs advertising products of the East and West vied for attention as the cab pushed farther into the crowded streets, and she wondered if this had been an error in judgment. Should she have gone directly to the airport? Were they on her trail even now? Or did they think her dead?

They.

She had been running from the faceless they for too long.

She could see the Victorian elegance of a former British mansion, the timeless beauty of its stone exterior a sign that she was almost home. She took courage from the familiar sight as the building pushed its stately presence into a world that seemed to be fighting for space. It was as if it refused to relinquish the hold it once had had, standing rock solid as the world around it changed.

The cab swung around the corner and the landscape changed again. If there was anything she loved about Georgetown it was how the old laced its presence through the new, how British traditions merged with Malay. She had purposely taken an apartment relatively close to the school within the hustle and bustle of daily life in Georgetown. Her apartment was a low-slung building in a cluttered section of the city where shops and open-air stalls dotted the landscape and fronted the more traditional brick-and-mortar buildings behind them. She'd loved this area from the first moment she'd laid eyes on it.

Not today.

Today, even under the brilliant afternoon sun, it seemed flush with shadows. On the sidewalk a man walked in a djellaba as his leather sandals skimmed easily across the concrete. His wife walked by his side in her traditional burka, her face and her thoughts hidden from the world by a layer of cloth and a veil. It wasn't an uncommon sight in Georgetown. Yet today, despite the fact that he held her hand—it all seemed to take on a sinister edge. Erin turned away to look out the opposite window.

The cab pulled over, and as she opened the door, the scent of curry intermingled with the smell of sewer. It was familiar and had begun to remind her of home, of here. After two months Georgetown felt comfortable, safe. *Had*, she thought with regret.

"Could you wait, please?" she requested as she stepped out of the cab.

Inside the apartment building, the narrow hallway with its faded morning glory wallpaper was empty. Only the chatter of a television set coming through one door and the clunking of the ancient washing machine down the hall broke the quiet. She stopped at the dark wood door at the end of the hallway. For a minute it was as if she wasn't here, as if this nightmare had never happened.

Daniel, she thought, and a sob hitched deep inside her and threatened her control. She took a deep breath. She needed to focus on running, but she could only think of Daniel. He was one of the few friends she'd made in Georgetown, and he'd still be alive if she hadn't loaned him her car. He hadn't asked to borrow it any more than he'd asked to die. It had all been her fault.

Her fault. Those two words kept reeling through her mind.

Stop it, she told herself. *Just stop it*. Now wasn't the time for recriminations or even grieving. She had to get out before she jeopardized someone else's life.

Erin reached for the knob and hesitated. She ran her tongue along her bottom lip. She looked down at the key in her hand. This time when she reached she touched the heavy brass knob, but then dropped her hand and took a step back. A small knot of white tissue lay on the floor. She worried her fingers against her palms, staring at that tiny piece of tissue.

"Erin."

She jumped, bit back a shriek and swung around.

"Yong, you scared me."

"There was someone asking for you earlier today. Did they find you?" the apartment owner asked. His face was downcast, and his slight shoulders slouched as they always did. "I'm sorry. After he left I opened your door just to do a check. We've had to replace some of the locks in the building." He shrugged. "I didn't go in, but I wanted to make sure your lock was working, that it couldn't be easily compromised. Besides, I'm sorry if he was a friend of yours, but I didn't like the look of him. And a double check is never a bad idea."

She unclenched her hand and took a step back. "I thought someone had been here."

"I thought you might." He smiled. "The old tissue in the door frame trick. Not a bad idea for a single woman. Not that we have much trouble with break-ins but you never know." He cleared his throat, the sound raspy and raw in the narrow hallway. "Just glad you haven't needed it."

"Thanks, Yong. I don't know what I'd do without you."

"No trouble," Yong said, but his eyes narrowed and he took a step closer. "You're all right?"

"Fine. Thank you." She turned the key over in her hand.

"That doesn't sound fine to me. Remember, like I've said, you need anything. I have daughters your age. But you know that. You met one of them." He hesitated. "You're sure nothing's wrong?"

"I'm sure."

"Okay," he said and turned away, jingling keys in his hand.

"Yong."

"Yeah." He stopped.

"What did he look like? The man, I mean." She fumbled with words and struggled to keep the tremor out of her voice.

"A big guy, six feet, maybe more. Hard to tell from my view down here." He chuckled. "I don't know. Not bad-looking." He paused. "Why? You think you might know him?"

"Was he Malay?" she asked.

"Don't think so. Had an accent, not Aussie or anything. Something else."

"Thanks." She hadn't asked his hair color or his race or... Did it matter? She knew he wasn't Malay. If he got close enough for her to see him, did she stand a chance? She had to get out of here and fast. But she needed to know. She had to ask at least one of those questions. "What color was his hair?"

"Don't know. He was wearing one of those knitted caps."

He jangled his keys, his sneaker-clad feet almost twitching as he answered her. "Look, I don't think he'll be back. And I'll be keeping a closer eye on things."

Her hand shook as it went to the door frame.

"No worries," he said over his shoulder as he headed down the hallway and to his own apartment.

"No worries," she repeated.

She turned the key in the lock with fingers that still shook. She stood in the doorway for a minute, then two. She pushed the door open wider. Her eyes darted back and forth, taking in micro snapshots of the room. Behind her a door slammed, and she jumped.

Hesitantly, she leaned one hand against the door frame as if that would ground her, make everything normal or turn back the clock. But nothing changed. The cot folded down from the wall, the kitchenette was jammed against the opposite wall, the tiny television in the far corner. Through the narrow window that faced the street, she could see the cab waiting.

"This is it," she murmured. "This is goodbye." She wiped the back of her hands across both eyes. She took a breath and then another, pulled out a tissue and blew her nose.

She grabbed her bag from the top shelf of the closet, tore clothes from hangers and emptied her drawers. Within a few minutes she was packed.

She never looked back as she closed the door behind her, as if this was just another day, and hurried out the door and into the waiting cab.

"The airport, please," she said. Her hand knotted around the straps of her knapsack and a small bag that carried her few personal items as she perched on the edge of her seat. She pressed her free hand to her temple as if that would still the headache that was beginning to beat dully and then dropped it to clutch the seat in front of her.

JOSH SLIPPED OUT the back entrance of the school and tucked the brochure he'd stolen from her classroom into his pocket. He would disappear as silently as he had arrived, leaving the retreating flames and tamped-down chaos to the authorities. He glanced at his watch, which functioned as a GPS as well as registered the time among other things. He hadn't expected the car bomb. As a precaution, he'd planned to mount a small tracking device on her car that would have followed her anywhere she went.

The victim—collateral damage. It was the only way to think of such things without losing it. He'd seen a number of breakdowns in the field from either mental or emotional stress; he didn't plan to become one of them.

Collateral damage.

School caretaker. That information hadn't been too hard to obtain. He'd overheard the hysterical words of a female teacher, confirmed that the car was his target's and that she'd lent it out, confirmed that Erin Argon was still alive.

Would she flee by land or air? Where? He considered the trajectory of her five-month flight. She'd begun her flight fueled by fear and misguided advice rather than immediate danger. Lucky and wily, her changed name and Canadian passport had kept her hidden until these past few weeks when he had been assigned the case. Still, she was damn lucky, and he knew he had little time to find her before the Anarchists beat him to it.

Luck aside it was amazing what she had accomplished and how easily she had slipped out of sight. So far she had crossed no fewer than ten international borders. Other than the weeks in Singapore, this had been the only place where she had settled. So where would a woman go who had crossed continents and countries, who had thought she was safe and who now had to come up with an alternate plan?

He was under her skin. An inkling of doubt rose at that thought. Doubt that maybe it was the other way around. He shrugged it off. She was an assignment, nothing more. He'd studied her, he knew her. She was tired. She'd go somewhere to regroup, to come up with a plan and another place to hide, because this time she had run, more than likely, without a plan. Where would she go? He touched the brochure in his pocket and wondered if it could be as easy as that.

"It's a risk," he muttered and smiled. There wasn't anything better than a risk; throw in one of his infamous hunches and he was betting that he was bang on right. After all, who else would know that she was fascinated by Malaysia's bat caves in Gunung Mulu National Park? He was guessing she had kept that information to herself. He certainly wouldn't have suspected it if she hadn't left her canvas satchel and run, taking nothing from her classroom but her purse. And if he hadn't snuck into her classroom before he left he would never have known, either, for he would never have found her brochure on the Mulu Caves and literally stumbled on to where he was now sure she planned to go next.

He jumped in a cab and gave the driver the order for

the airport even as his mind churned through the options. She was panicked. Would she take the slow route out of here or just hop a plane? He suspected the latter. If she were smart, and so far she'd proven she was, a few transfers around the country and her trail would become a little grayer, a little more difficult to follow. Keep on doing that and she could disappear. He needed to get to the airport to confirm he was right and get a ticket on that same plane. He leaned back.

"Damn," he muttered as his thoughts went back to the one man she'd reached out to, the man who had been the catalyst to send Erin Kelley Argon on her five-month flight.

"Mike Olesk, we finally meet."

He held out his hand.

"I don't have time for this," the grizzle-faced burnout said.

"You used to be a city cop," Josh said.

"What's it to you?"

"I'm with the CIA." He held out his identification.

"And you want to know about Erin."

Josh's lips tightened. "I didn't expect it would be this easy," he said drily. *He seriously hadn't thought the man would admit to knowing her, never mind that he would just blurt out her name.*

"That's about all I'm going to tell you," he said with a surly edge to his voice.

"She's in danger," Josh said. *"And you have the power to help me find her."*

"How do I know you are who you say you are?"

"I could get a warrant," he said, but it was only a mild threat.

"You don't have time now, do you? The trial begins in a little more than a month. They need Erin, and the

Anarchists need her dead. She's the witness that can put them all away." Mike shook his head.

"Why?"

"As if you don't know. She witnessed a murder, and it wasn't just any murder, was it? No, the gang leader up and shoots what looks like the gang's link to crime-based money out of Europe." He ran a hand through hair that shone with grease. *"You're not the only one in the know, and you're not the only one hunting Erin."*

"How well do you know her?" Josh asked quietly. There was something else going on here or at least he suspected so. Information was flowing too quickly, and that, he had learned during his six years in the field, was always suspect.

Mike looked surprised and there was a secretive cast to his bloodshot brown eyes. *"Not that well. I knew her as a kid when her father and I worked together. As an adult, we lost touch until... Well, until she came to me for help."*

"And you helped her disappear."

"Something like that. But I don't know where she is now. I haven't heard from her in months."

"Fourteen days," he muttered as outside the traffic continued to flash by. That was the number of days since he had spoken to Mike Olesk, and then had cobbled together her flight path that had taken him to Singapore and finally to this point.

Mulu Caves in Gunung Mulu National Park. He opened the brochure. The glossy pictures would have been enticing in another situation. The information gave the usual condensed and carefully edited descriptions, all of it what he already knew. The park was isolated and accessible only by a ten-hour boat ride or a small plane. It was the perfect place to hide, but it was also the perfect place for a trap. He suspected she hadn't thought of that; she hadn't had time.

He looked out the window and smiled.

She was in his sights. He wasn't in hers.

Chapter Five

In the past hour Josh had laid a false trail from Miri, Malaysia, through Beijing and then to Hong Kong, a hotel registration here in Erin Kelley's name, a car rental there. But that trail would delay the men who were after her only for so long—a day, maybe two.

"They're offering ten million for the kill, Josh." Vern folded his arms, his feet propped on the desk, his florid skin at odds with his blond hair. *"Fortunately, the first man out of the gate isn't one of the best."*

The passage of time since that conversation seemed nominal considering all that had transpired. Josh shifted his pack and artfully dodged milling passengers in Miri's airport, all the while taking in the change in her appearance. Despite the fact that her new hair color gleamed a startling blue black and wire-rimmed glasses glinted beneath the artificial light and hid her vivid blue eyes, he still recognized her. Her frame was thinner, more fragile than her pictures had indicated, and the blue-black wig made her delicate skin look pale and gave the illusion of fragility. It was an amateurish attempt at a quick disguise, but it was effective for now. In fact, the black hair color was genius in a population where the average person was dark haired and dark skinned. It made her blend in just a bit more. Unfortunately, she hadn't had time or hadn't thought of the pallor of her skin accentuated against the unnaturally dark hair.

He shrugged. It would do and sometimes on the run, that was all you had. He imagined she'd be pulling out hair dye when they reached the Gunung Mulu National Park. It wasn't a bad idea and it was all he had or, he amended, she had, at least until he developed some kind of rapport with her.

Erin Kelley Argon.

He had followed her flight halfway across the world and watched her survive despite the odds. Her path hadn't been as simple to pick up as he'd first thought it would be. He'd been surprised at every turn. At times she'd shown gut intelligence for flight, as if she had done this at some other time in her life. Despite having help and advice from Mike Olesk, alone she had still gone through the steps with a polish that hadn't left one misstep. That was evident in the fact that the Anarchists hadn't expanded their search off the continental United States until shortly before he'd been deployed.

Yet nothing in the history he had gone over said she had ever had a reason to run, to hide. Until the murder, she'd led a normal life.

He was still in awe of those initial moments of her disappearance. Her flight had been brilliant, classic even. She'd put everything in place before running. She'd left San Diego and legally changed her name, dropped her last name while still in the country and in a matter of weeks had obtained a passport in her new name and country. And when she'd run, she hadn't flown but instead had zigzagged north into Canada and taken a train across that country. But what he'd least expected was the creativity that followed. She'd jumped a container ship and taken a convoluted path before finally arriving in Eastern Europe.

He had followed her journey as he had prepared for this assignment with an almost morbid fascination. She had kept him awake nights as he'd admired the ingenuity this woman had put into her escape.

A movement caught his eye.

She was at the ticket counter. He took a step forward, his gaze locked on her and then veered left. He had to transform from Josh Sedovich, CIA agent, to just Josh, tourist. He headed to the washroom and his own change of appearance.

ERIN TOOK A deep breath as she tried to portray a casual traveler. It wasn't easy considering everything that had happened. This was the third flight since this morning's tragedy. She was lucky there had been room on the flight to Miri, and now she hoped her luck would hold out again on the flight to the Gunung Mulu National Park and its legendary caves.

"Just made it."

The voice behind her was male and too close.

She turned to face a shock of dark curly hair and brown eyes that sparkled with humor, yet something more serious seemed to lurk there. He was clean-shaven and attractive in a boyish kind of way. Still, she took an involuntary step back even as she took in his knee-length beige shorts and white T-shirt with Kuala Lumpur's skyline emblazoned across it. Only an overly enthusiastic tourist would actually wear a T-shirt like that, never mind the socks. Yet in this world, her new world, nothing was a given. Nothing was as it appeared and no one was safe. It had been a harsh reminder, today's lesson—short and brutal. She blinked back tears. She had to act as if everything was normal, as if she was no different than anyone else.

She offered him a half smile.

"You did," she agreed as she assessed and discarded the man behind her. She'd never seen him before and his dress screamed tourist. He was no threat.

She turned away as the couple ahead of her moved from the counter and the clerk motioned her forward. She stepped up, dutifully provided her weight and that of her luggage, and within minutes was checked in.

"When do we board?" she asked.

The clerk swung around to where a clock face ticked the minutes. It was two o'clock. "Fifteen minutes," he replied. "Through that gate."

Outside the tarmac made this morning's classroom feel cool. Heat shimmered and distorted the landscape. Even the low-lying shrubs that skirted the edges of the pavement appeared to be wilting in the heat. The distant hills rose in a scalloped frame of shadowed images that were fronted by patches of emerald-green forests and stretches of clay in hues of rust. Ahead of her stood a small prop plane with Malaysia emblazed in red and blue lettering on its narrow metal frame.

As they lined up to board the plane, Erin could feel every breath and her heart seemed to thump loud enough to be heard.

"It's hot today, again. Odd," she muttered.

"Excuse me?" the man with the so-uncool T-shirt asked.

"Oh, I… I'm sorry. I was talking to myself. Bad habit."

"Traveling alone does it to one. Do it myself," he said cheerfully.

"I suppose." She tried to keep her attention on him. She eased her hold on her bags.

"A way to self-medicate," he said. "Talking to oneself. At least, so I was told. Not sure what exactly one is medicating, but there it is—self-help. All I know."

"Thanks," she said with what she hoped was a smile. She pushed a strand of hair out of her eyes and felt the sweat that she knew must be glistening on her forehead.

"It is unusually hot," he added.

She offered a half smile and held back as he and the others inched forward, waiting for bags to be loaded.

"Next!"

A bag was thrown onto the scale.

A heavyset man followed the suitcase, stepping onto the scale.

It was a pattern—weigh luggage, weigh passenger.

"Small plane—they have to juggle the weight." It was T-shirt man, as she'd begun to think of him.

"Next."

"After you," he said and accompanied his words with a slight sweep of his hand motioning her forward as they reached the front of the line.

"Thank you." Her hand tightened on her bags and she blinked and blinked again. She bit her lip and her hand stopped shaking. She turned her attention to him, noticing that he was taller than she'd first thought, but his broad build gave the illusion of a shorter frame. As she'd determined before, he was good-looking, but more than likely a bit of a goof if his souvenir T-shirt, too-long shorts and tennis shoes with socks were any indication. Yet he wasn't as boyish-looking as she had thought. In fact, he wasn't boyish-looking at all. In the sunlight, his features were almost craggy in a roguish kind of way.

"No worries," he said.

"No worries," she repeated.

She glanced around as she took her seat. No additional passengers, just the same ones she'd already accounted for. There was no one who might pose a threat. The passengers included an older couple with a slight camera addiction, judging from the camera bags that dangled around both their necks. Both carried a few extra pounds that were not the well-toned form she assumed would be required of a hit man. She shuddered at the thought.

She'd come close, too close.

She turned her attention back to the occupants of the small plane. The other couple, both male, was obviously excited about the trip and even more obviously in love. Both were slight and short in stature, and effeminate, one more than the other. Definitely not hit men material. No threat there, either. She folded her arms under her chest and looked out the window, but instead her thoughts went to the past and her family.

"You can't leave us Erin." Tears swam in Sarah's eyes.

"There's no choice, Sarah. You can't breathe a word of what happened."

"But Erin, you can't leave. I won't let you."

"There's no choice," she repeated as she put an arm around her sister, hugging her close. *"You're pregnant and that changes everything."*

"You said I was a fool," Sarah said. *"And you were right."*

"The baby's real, Sarah. And whether I agree with your decisions in getting to this state, or who you chose to have a baby with..."

"Father absentee," Sarah muttered. *"I think I'm off men, possibly for life."*

"I'll protect you both, and the only way to do that is for me to get out of here."

"But your job?"

"Not permanent. I'm substituting at a variety of schools."

"But you love the kids. You live for your work."

"There's no other choice, Sarah. If I don't leave the Anarchists will hunt us down."

"Instead, they'll only hunt you," Sarah said sadly. "I can't talk you out of this insanity?"

"You can't." She hugged Sarah. "We'll be in touch."

"I love you, sis," Sarah said.

The engine vibrated the small plane, and as it cut into a turn that seemed to shift passengers and luggage alike, Erin held her breath.

She pinched her fingers together, her nails biting into skin. She looked out the window. Beneath them the forest canopy sprawled in lush greenery hugging ragged limestone cliffs that punctured the jungle floor with primitive ease. The forest appeared endless, and for a brief moment Erin allowed herself to be caught up in the natural beauty of this place. While her gut tightened as she remembered that she'd be isolated, alone and only temporarily safe, temporarily out of sight. She needed a plan and she needed it quickly.

"Completely awesome, isn't it?" said the man who had waited in line behind her.

"It is," she agreed as ahead of them the two couples admired the view out their respective windows, the two men silently watching the passing scenery, and the husband and wife taking an endless stream of pictures.

"Name's Josh," he said easily.

"Erin," she supplied reluctantly. So far she'd managed to dodge conversation with any of the other passengers. She looked at him. She had to be sure he was no threat. She reminded herself that if he were out to kill her, he would have done so, unless, of course, he was waiting for the plane to land and for anonymity. But if that were the case, he wouldn't have been wearing that ridiculous T-shirt.

You're seeing danger where none exists, she told herself. Still, she had to make sure he was safe. Nothing in his demeanor suggested a threat of any kind. But she'd learned early on that danger came quickly and unexpectedly.

How long would it be safe to stay here? She knew the answer even as she asked the question. Not long, a matter of days until she got a plan together. She had to get out of Malaysia, get across the border to another country and safety. She needed to sketch a path, a number of flights within the border, before leaving Malaysia for good. She needed a plan and a map, and she had fled without either.

She took a deep, shaky breath. It had been a huge misjudgment, an error. She had thought she was safe. She had let down her guard. Now one innocent person was dead and she was running without direction.

"Something wrong?" Josh leaned forward, concern reflected in the furrows in his forehead.

Damn, she thought. He'd been watching her and she hadn't noticed.

"You're afraid of flying?"

The roar of the engine seemed to fill the small cabin.

She wished that was all it was. Instead of replying, she remained with her gaze riveted on the window and on land—a new challenge.

"We're about to land. See." He pointed. "It won't be long. You'll be fine."

"I..." She began to assure him and to deny any fear of flying, and then stopped. The new Erin could not afford to offer too much information, too much familiarity. Lies were her new truth. It had taken her months to become comfortable with that, and still it rang false. She still had to remind herself. Lies weren't who she was. The old Erin had been open, trusting, honest... No more. She took a breath, put a smile on her face and met him head-on. "Thank you. This whole small plane thing makes me a bit queasy."

"Used to do the same to me," he agreed. But this time when he looked at her there was something darker and more intense in the look that seemed to belie the flippancy that had seemed second nature to him.

She shivered.

"Are you cold?" This time his brows almost met over the question.

"I'm fine."

The plane began its descent and the afternoon sun gleamed on the dense greenery, adding a sparkle-like affect. Another time it might have been amazing. Now, she could feel Josh's eyes on her. She sighed. That was all she needed—a man's interest.

Or did she?

She shifted in her seat and eyed him from the corner of her eye. A plan began to form. Her hand drifted to the window frame. She was a woman alone, on the run. That was what they were looking for. That was how she had left. An American posing as a Canadian, one who taught school and didn't fit here. They'd looked in the school-yards, and they'd found her.

Once.

They'd find her again.

Traveling alone made her stand out. She had to change her name again and her identity, but right in this moment, there was nothing to do but forge ahead with who she had become. But there was something she could change.

She looked over at Josh, and he smiled almost hope-fully.

Maybe that was the best cover of all. She hated being alone, yet, oddly, she had become used to it. While she didn't like it, she didn't feel as uncomfortable as she had in the beginning. Of course, the beginning had been laced with so much fear. The fear was still there, but it was like white noise, something that had become her daily companion, a familiar entity that reminded her not to trust.

She'd trusted and Daniel had died.

Chapter Six

Josh stepped onto the metal stairs of the plane's exit ramp. He was right behind Erin, her black wig gleaming like a beacon in the late-afternoon sun. He looked to the right and left as he matched his steps to hers. The tarmac stretched out, cut through the relentless jungle that closed in around them. The resort was built well above the ground and away from the unpredictability of nature in a satellite of stilt-legged buildings adjoined by wooden walkways. It was rustic in an elegant fashion.

"Heard the king of Monaco stayed here. Or maybe it was a prince. Not sure, royalty of some kind," the older woman with a camera dangling from a leather strap around her neck said to the man who stood beside her sporting a camera of his own.

A resort that had housed royalty, Josh thought. That was new since he last visited, and reassuring. The logistics of security had already been tested.

While he considered these things, his attention never turned from Erin. He was aware of every movement, of the fact that she now stood in line just ahead of him. He watched as her fingernails scraped against the strap of a small canvas bag, making an odd rough-edged sound, the only sign that she was nervous.

His gaze shifted slightly ahead of her to the couple

closest to them, and his biggest concern because of that, because of proximity. They had matching hard-shelled suitcases on wheels—oversized and, he suspected, over-packed. The luggage was a fairly good indicator that this trip was the most risky of their travels, for the luggage almost screamed safe and their demeanor capped his assessment. They were no threat.

There was a low hum of chatter around them as the passengers stared at the amazing backdrop the distant cliffs made as they pierced their off-white talons through the lush green jungle. He watched the tourists, listening to what they said, how they interacted with each other, mentally recording all. It was humans who would cause any problems in the future, not scenery. Because of that, he didn't care for limestone peaks or bat caves except as a strategic means of escape, places to hide if the worst-case scenario occurred. In the meantime, what he cared about were the nooks and crannies where an assassin could lurk. Again, he scoured the disembarking passengers and moved on to the resort crew that waited on the edge of the empty runway with a minivan to take those less limber up to the resort.

His gaze slid over the employee at the head of the line. The man was lean, sun-bronzed and approximately five foot four. He was dressed in pristine white cotton pants and a T-shirt with the Royal Mulu Resort logo emblazoned on it. Instinct told him he was no threat, but he'd wait to pass judgment once he had the evidence to back up that initial determination.

The last bag was unloaded and he saw Erin take a step toward it.

He hurried forward as she reached for an oversized knapsack.

"Let me take that." He lifted the bag as he made the

comment, leaving her no option but to graciously accept. "Mulu is more beautiful than the brochure promised."

She gave him a look that could only be called leery.

"I never anticipated this." He swept his arm in a half circle. "Did you?" He didn't even consider how inane the comment was. It didn't fit who he was, but it fit his current persona. He'd just have to watch it so as not to go overboard with it.

"It is, but then that's why I came here. As I imagine you did, too."

"Actually," he said, "I'd never heard of Mulu until a friend enlightened me. I didn't even make a reservation." He shrugged. "I don't like to travel like that, but…"

"No reservation? Really?"

She only looked mildly interested and far from trusting.

"Did you reserve ahead?" he asked and felt her eyes on her bag.

"Yes, of course." She frowned. Her eyes narrowed as they met his and her lips were compressed in a fine line. "You are lucky it's October. One of the few months where there's less tourists." She held out her hand for her bag.

"You're sure? I can take it."

Her hand brushed his. Something shifted in her gaze and her lips softened.

"It's heavy. Let me," he said.

"Thanks," she replied as she led the way with a determined and slight sway to her hips, which despite her slim figure were seductively curvy.

Overhead a bird screeched. The shadow of the bird's startled flight cut across them as it dove, giving a view of glossy black tail feathers before it disappeared into the lush jungle. She jumped and slipped on the wooden walkway, which was slick from a recent rain. He took her arm, steadying her.

"Careful," he warned as she looked at him with an expression of fear mixed with gratitude. There was a haunted look in her eyes, or maybe he imagined it, for the look was as quickly gone, and replaced by the determination he'd seen earlier, an emotion that consistently emanated from her.

"I can take it now." She reached for her bag.

"You're sure. There's no need…"

Their eyes clashed, and he handed her bag to her. "I could have taken it the rest of the way."

"You could have," she agreed. "But I prefer not."

She gave him a smile that took some of the edge off her words, and then turned with the bag slung over her shoulder, the straps gripped with one white-knuckled hand as she followed the two men who were already a few yards ahead. Two minutes later he was holding open the glass-plated door to the reception area for her as a rush of air-conditioning swirled around them.

"Well, we're here," he said as he graciously waited for the woman behind him to enter before relinquishing the door to a heavyset gray-haired man who was towing a wheeled suitcase behind him.

"We are," she said over her shoulder and strode determinedly toward the reception desk without a backward glance.

"We have you booked for a double occupancy." The desk clerk looked up and then over at Josh as if he were the missing double. "As you requested."

"That's right," Erin said. "My boyfriend will be joining me later." Her eyes slid to Josh and her hand slipped through the strap of the bag. Her eyes flitted to where a round, white-faced clock hummed on the wall behind the reception desk.

Four o'clock.

She sneaked another peek at Josh and saw only admiration in his gaze. Despite the wire-rimmed glasses and tacky T-shirt, he wasn't as geeky as she'd first thought. In fact, there was something about him that she couldn't quite put her finger on. She gathered her passport and held it in an iron grip.

She looked away but felt his eyes on her.

"Boyfriend?" he asked, disappointment etching his words.

She nodded as her gaze flitted to his. There was an intensity there, a knowing that belied the unbecoming tourist T-shirt. There was smoke in his eyes that seemed to pierce through the lens of his black-rimmed glasses and a ruggedness to the face behind the frames.

"This place is amazing," he said as he turned and looked one way and then the other, clearly overwhelmed. She suspected he was an infrequent traveler.

Her lips twitched, and she almost smiled.

"I'll see you around," she said as she left him to check in and followed the concierge out the door.

Five minutes later she scanned her room for exits. The airy, sunlit room held a wicker desk and chair and a comfortable-looking queen-size bed, but those were minor points. What was important were the window, the door and what was outside. From what she could see, barring the front entrance, the only exit was the window that looked out onto a narrow catwalk, a thin bamboo walkway that might have been used by resort employees. She glanced at the window. It would do in an emergency. First she had to determine if she could open it or if she would need to break the glass. If the latter were the case, she would need something handy to break the glass with.

She opened the stained bamboo closet door. Inside was nothing but a row of old-fashioned wire hangers. She ran a thumb over one, thinking that these hangers could be used as a weapon if necessary. They weren't much, but they'd be better than facing any threat empty-handed.

Her hand quivered. Whoever was after her was more sophisticated than coat hangers. They'd blown up a car. They meant business, and they meant to kill her. It was as Mike had said and she hadn't wanted to believe—only worse. A slight headache began to pulse low in the base of her skull. She missed her friends, her family, her apartment—and she missed her cat.

She'd delivered Edgar to her sister the day before she'd run. Sarah had been sworn to silence and Mike to vigilance. They'd both be fine. The cat would be well cared for, spoiled and more than likely a few pounds over his ideal weight by the time she got home, and her sister would have had the baby she shouldn't be having. A single woman with no career aspirations and no man willing to stick around wasn't the ideal candidate for motherhood. But that was Erin's opinion, not Sarah's.

Home.

Her thumbnail pinched into the palm of her hand.

"Focus," she reminded herself as the wave of homesickness, loss and despair washed through her. She took her mind from other places back to the moment and to reworking the plan. She couldn't worry about family or friends or even cats; there was nothing she could do for them but stay away and stay alive.

She looked at the closet, closed the doors and went through her list of defenses. The list was meager. She had pepper spray from a night market stall. Other than a self-defense course she'd taken with another primary grade teacher, she had little in her favor.

As she thought through the events of the past few days, she realized that she had to get out of the country in a very short time. This escape was only temporary. She didn't know how good the people hired to find her were, but she suspected they might be very good. They'd found the school she'd worked in, they'd found her new identity and they'd attempted to kill her.

"Stay calm," she reminded herself. But there seemed no end in sight and no one she could approach for help.

She looked at her watch as if that would give her the answers that weren't forthcoming.

Her headache was escalating.

She sat down on the bed. She'd run three quarters of the way around the globe and they'd found her. She'd changed her appearance yet again. And she'd been on a cash-only basis since leaving home. She needed to do more.

She wasn't sure where she was going next, but she knew what she needed in the short term while she was here.

Her nails bit into the palms of her hands. She relaxed her hands and took a breath—panicking would get her nowhere.

"Damn boyfriend dumped you," she murmured with a laugh that held no humor at all. "And then along came Josh." She hated every aspect of this story, from its very necessity to its needy woman overtones to using an innocent man—possibly toying with his affections. All of it was distasteful and all of it was necessary. She pulled a box of hair dye from her pack.

Josh Sedovich, an easy man to reel in. She thought that without arrogance but instead with the thoughts of an attractive woman who knew she was attractive.

She wouldn't hurt him, just engage in some harmless flirtation—the illusion of a couple.

She sucked in a deep breath. Her life was an illusion, an illusion that hurt.

Chapter Seven

Josh shielded his eyes. Despite the threat of rain later in the day, the sun beat hot and relentless even in late afternoon. This was the least popular time of year, as the rain made things muggy and uncomfortable. It wasn't usual for numbers to drop too much, but with renovations on some of the more distant accommodations, tourism was noticeably down. That was good news—less activity to monitor, fewer potential incoming threats.

The drone of a plane's engine pierced the sultry heat. It was on schedule. He watched as the plane landed.

He'd just gotten word that, as he had suspected, the last hit had been by one of the Anarchists's gang members. Bobbie Xavier was not the brightest tool in the shed, but he was one of the deadliest. Josh had gotten confirmation that his diversion had worked. Bobbie was on his way to Hong Kong.

But with the recent news the stakes had just gone up. The Anarchists had hired someone else, a man who wouldn't work in tandem with Bobbie, and one who wouldn't depend on luck or the mistakes of a woman who had never had to disappear before. The man was a professional. He had a record of success that ended in a trail of death, and he had a record of outsourcing. That meant the numbers on her trail could and more likely would, go up.

That meant that there might not just be one. In the near future, there might be two or three. They needed to get out of here, maybe sooner than he'd previously thought.

Sid Mylo was not someone to take lightly. Why the hell were they hiring someone with Sid's capabilities to go after someone like Erin? Sure, she had been on the run for five months, but—and that was the next mystery— why had it taken them that long to send someone after her? Until now they had depended on the muscle of the various club members across the states as the alert had gone out and the nets had gone up. But they hadn't looked outside the continental United States.

"Erin Argon," he muttered. It was the real woman he would be bringing back, not the actress Erin Kelley. He wondered how she could have gotten herself into this mess. She didn't look like the type to date bikers. But that was exactly what she'd done.

He knew some women got off on that. Some dated criminals slated for death row, sought out men who were bent on destruction, their own as well as that of others. But it was rather disconcerting to think that a primary-school teacher would spend her free time with men who had questionable ethics. Drug dealers, pimps and mur- derers—and that was only the beginning of the crimes that could be attributed to various members of the Anar- chists. It didn't seem to fit anything he knew about her. And whether she'd learned her lesson after one colos- sal mistake, he didn't know. Only she knew that. And it wasn't something he needed to know. That knowledge would no more save her than hiding out in Mulu would.

He pulled open the door of the hotel lobby.

The concierge stood by the desk. His brown pants and jacket seemed to fade into the background. But his posture and wide smile, despite his solid but short stature, made him immediately stand out.

Their eyes met and held in a moment of understanding before the concierge looked away.

Josh waited a few minutes, glancing through a display of pamphlets before turning to the concierge. "Must be nice to work here."

He looped his thumbs into the belt loops of his shorts. In listening range was an older couple that seemed to be involved in their own discussion, but they glanced over at him with what he thought of as a tourist's curiosity.

"Yes, sir." The concierge met his gaze this time with a rather puzzled expression, as if he didn't know where the question was leading.

"Josh." He held out his hand. "Three," he mouthed. It was the number of days, maximum, that he planned to stay before getting Erin out of here.

"Tenuk," the concierge said with a rather solemn grace and tapped his finger silently, one, two, three. It was confirmation, nothing else.

Josh moved to the back of the lobby. His gaze grazed the bank of pamphlets against one wall while he kept a discreet eye on the comings and goings of staff and guests in the lobby.

The woman behind the desk was reading, but she shoved the book under the counter as the door opened, announcing more guests. An older couple checked in with more noise and fluff than their entrance warranted. The man was balding and sweating, the woman was thick set, easily as tall as the man, and both carried themselves in a way that spoke of never having been denied.

There was nothing more to be learned here. Josh dropped the pamphlet, glanced briefly at Tenuk and opened the door.

Outside, he lowered his sunglasses. The polarized lenses provided some privacy, hiding his eyes from scrutiny. It was ninety-two degrees, hotter than normal. He moved away from the hotel entrance and to the side where he could discreetly watch the new arrivals.

He pushed the ball cap he'd just purchased in the gift shop off his forehead and wiped at a nonexistent line of sweat. About one hundred feet away a couple sat at an outdoor bar drinking what looked like a highball of some sort—rum and Coke, he suspected.

The reception door opened with a slightly gritty sound that spoke of a need of attention, adjustment of the hinges possibly. Tenuk came up beside him. The two of them stood there for a moment in silence, taking in the comings and goings of the resort and their position in it.

"Is the flight that just arrived from Miri also the last flight out?" Josh asked. It was a pointless question meant only to cloud their real purpose should anyone be listening. He already knew the answer; both of them did. There wasn't anything about the resort's transportation that he hadn't been briefed on. What he didn't know were the people who worked here or the guests who were currently in residence. Or, more importantly, those who might be in transit to the resort.

"There are two more."

Josh nodded.

"Your accommodation is acceptable, sir?" His sun-bronzed face was scarred and pockmarked, his frame small but solid. Tenuk Laksana was one of the best of Malaysia's special forces, or so Josh has been told.

"Of course. Exactly as I expected. Better," he said with enthusiasm.

"It's clear," Tenuk said as he leaned sideways against the railing.

"One plane in since ours," he said. Behind them was jungle, in front was a supply cabin and farther away he could see the glimmer of the pool. At the far end of the resort a couple threw a ball for their toddler, and in the pool a heavyset woman was doing laps.

"Another expected in half an hour. I double-checked the roster. A group of senior tourists arriving from Bangkok." He shoved his hands in his pockets. "Six in all and on the next roster, four young women who are scheduled to begin work here tomorrow."

"The wild cards are the dormitories," Josh said, referring to the hostels that housed backpackers in a dormitory-style room.

"True enough. That's where the budget travelers stay, and there's usually more of them. Fortunately, you have luck on your side. The home stay and dormitory are closed for maintenance."

"Manageable," Josh replied. "If we'd had to deal with the home stays..." He thought of the area where locals managed various types of tourist accommodation just outside the main resort, and where many were under renovation as a result of the park's recent accommodation safety mandates. "Despite the season, the tourism would have increased."

"Meaning more security issues. Still, even without them it's a rough assignment," Tenuk said with a smile.

"Seen worse," he said shortly.

"Maybe, but she's lucky to still be alive."

Josh couldn't disagree with that. Fortunately, he'd found her before her luck had run out. If it hadn't been for her slips, it would have taken longer, but making friends in Singapore had been her first error. Emma Whyte was in a morgue because of her association with Erin Kelley Argon. It wasn't a pretty fact, but it was one that separated the professional from the amateur. A professional never would have made that mistake.

"Ten million," Tenuk hissed under his breath. "That's a lot of money, and I imagine the ante could go up. Where the hell are the Anarchists getting that kind of money?"

Josh ran a thumb along the railing. They were alone in this far corner of the resort. No one could hear this conversation, and still he was reluctant to say. If Tenuk didn't know where the money was coming from, it wasn't up to him to fill in the gaps.

"Word has it that their reach has stretched into Europe," Tenuk said. He laced his fingers together, cracked his knuckles. He dropped his hands and shrugged his shoulders. "The trial should prove interesting."

Josh nodded. "An understatement."

"They're flush with money. We're having problems here, too."

"This trial could be a watershed."

"You hope," Tenuk said. "They're getting a stream of funding from somewhere, and with the leader about to go on trial, anything could happen. Any way you look at it, the authorities need to cut off the funds."

"Can't disagree." Josh nodded.

"This witness can put a stop to it all. If the Anarchists' leader is nailed for Enrique's murder…" Tenuk rubbed his chin. "The murder of a European billionaire provides that link, proof even, especially when the murderer was the leader of the Anarchists."

"She couldn't have got caught up with worse," Josh agreed.

"The change of name was smart, but the ability to acquire a Canadian passport was a fortuitous stroke of luck on her part," Tenuk said thoughtfully.

"Unfortunately, the smokescreen wasn't deep enough. She's run out of time."

"Yeah, true enough. She's an amateur who didn't know she needed to change her skin more than once." Tenuk shifted and turned around to look into the jungle. "So far it's all clear. Not sure how long this window will stay open." He swung back around. "The killer running gave her some breathing space. I suppose it really gave the Anarchists room, as well. They weren't feeling any heat." He chuckled at his own joke. "Never suspected she'd left the States, did they?"

"Nope," Josh agreed.

"And now they have. I don't envy your job," Tenuk said. "A biker gang and your own FBI both desperate to find her. And you, man, where does that put you?"

Right in the middle, Josh thought. "On the firing line," he said as he turned away, his mouth a straight line as he gazed into the seemingly impermeable jungle.

"But I suspect that's where you like to be."

"And you don't?" Josh replied flatly, his attention shifting back to Tenuk.

"I suppose." Tenuk shrugged.

"Is the plane ready?"

"Plane?"

"Today, tomorrow and then out. Enough time to gain her trust, although earlier would be better. Considering how she is, what she knows, that might not be possible."

Tenuk looked pained. "This is the first I'm hearing of it."

"Nothing was arranged." There was a flat edge to his words and his mind ran through the ramifications of the oversight. "Vern was going to handle it."

"You're sure?"

He hadn't followed up. There hadn't been time. He

began to rework the possibilities. They couldn't stay any longer. He'd get in touch with Vern immediately. Too much time here was risky. "What's the word from George-town?"

"The disappearance of a local teacher and the explosion has made news." Tenuk pushed back from the railing. "That doesn't give you, or us, much time. There's a lot of money up for grabs." He rubbed his thumb against his chin. "Another mistake like the last and she's dead. Getting too close to people and then the car…" He shook his head. "She's lucky."

Josh couldn't disagree with that. But he understood what she'd done and why she'd done it, too. The need for stability, a place to call home—the need to blend. But she had blended too well. She'd blended right into sight.

Chapter Eight

Josh looked at his watch.

Six o'clock. They'd landed over two hours ago and he was now established in a room three doors from hers.

Dinnertime.

He pushed the empty bag of peanuts aside and stood up. Outside there was silence. He sat back down.

His mind shifted to the faulty intelligence that had brought her to this point.

There'd been a spotty internet trail. Other than a few communications out of a Thai resort four months ago that unfortunately for Emma Whyte had led to Singapore, there had been nothing. Only silence. But it had been enough to give him a direction and a continent: Asia.

"You're on your last legs," he murmured.

He put on the glasses and pulled on the baseball cap emblazoned with the words Mulu Caves. He angled the hat, tipping it slightly back from his face.

He grabbed what they called a man-purse or satchel. To him it was a purse, a distasteful and currently useful accessory. He slung it over his shoulder. He glanced in the mirror. If one didn't look at his buff arms or notice his tan, and if he kept his lips softened to detract from the hard line of his chin, he could pass as a typical tourist. No threat.

There was the distinct click of a door being opened. He

glanced at the monitor strapped to his wrist. It looked like a regular watch but it was far from that. It could function as speakers for a listening device, act as a GPS and still tell time. It also could be programmed for myriad other things, which he hadn't had time to configure before he'd been on the road for this assignment.

He stood up, gave her a minute or two to get a jump on him, and then opened the door. The heat of the afternoon had shifted to a muggy feel, and the earthy smell of rain permeated the air. But the rain was only a fine mist, warm and balmy. He began a leisurely walk along the wooden decking that bordered the cottages and fed them all into the main areas of the resort.

He turned the corner at the end of the line of cottages just as she entered the dining room. He took his time, looking here and there, running a finger along the wooden railway and all the time covertly watching.

Josh frowned as he reassessed the dining area for the second time that day. Natural light spilled in through a bank of windows that lined every side of the rectangular building. If there were trouble, there was little to no protection there. His hand went to the collar on his golf shirt and he adjusted one lapel so that it stood up slightly. The material clung in the heat and itched uncomfortably. The glasses slid and he pushed them back up with his thumb.

He reached for the door, gave the glass plate a push just as a shadow passed behind him.

Josh spun around, dropping his hand and touching the handle of his gun.

There was no one there. Yet someone had been. He'd felt it with an instinct that was rarely wrong.

There was movement to his left.

He shifted, turning sideways, presenting a smaller target as he scanned the resort. Four older couples in the distance, standing around—probably having a conversation about what they were going to do tomorrow.

Not the problem. He'd seen them come in.

His gaze went to where two men were talking, their voices raised and slightly slurred.

Something shifted again and seemed to move in the rapidly dwindling light. It was in the forest that bracketed this raised resort. That was where the trouble was, where he had always known it would be. He just hadn't expected it so soon.

Branches bent and twisted as a nearby tree shifted in a slight breeze. He eased forward, ready to confront, ready to—

A woman screamed.

He swung around and saw the same three backpackers he'd seen earlier, twentysomethings who were staying at the resort tonight. Tenuk had told him it was a one-night splurge. They weren't the problem. He could see that in the freeze frame in which they stood, as they turned startled faces in the direction of the scream.

He dropped his hand and headed toward the group and the origin of the scream.

"I've got this." It was Tenuk. His hand rested briefly on his arm, staying him. "I think I have an idea what the problem is. Nothing serious. Go have supper."

Josh watched Tenuk disappear among the backpackers, who seemed to overwhelm him in size and appeared as though they could easily overpower him. That was if Tenuk were a man of ordinary means, but as a member of Malaysian Special Forces he could take down a man or two with ease, just using his hands.

He stood there for a minute, a frown on his face as the backpackers scattered and he had a clear view as Tenuk spoke to the screaming woman and gestured to the ground. Even in the gathering dusk, Josh could see the problem. It was now clear that the scream had been nothing but the woman coming in unexpected contact with the resort's mascot—a foot-long gecko.

Tenuk. He'd appeared out of nowhere. As if he'd been watching Josh.

He stood there for a minute, maybe two, just watching—thinking, gathering information.

Finally, he turned and strode the short distance to the dining room. He opened the door and entered the large space. The windows he had noticed earlier ran the length of two walls and seemed to frame the second exit on the far side of the room. Tropical trees filled the northeast and southwest corners. The room was over half-full, and he noted approvingly that Erin had taken a seat by one of the potted plants, nearest the exit, as well as the kitchen.

He folded his hands behind his back and scanned the room, checking out each of the occupants, hoping the image he presented was that of a regular diner scouting out a table.

At the opposite corner and farthest away was a sixty-ish couple, leaning forward and deep in conversation, a bottle of wine listing in a wine bucket beside them. To the right and fifteen feet away was the couple he'd watched check in not two hours ago. They chatted with another couple, who appeared to be in their midforties and whom he'd already filed as nonthreatening. In the center was a family with two small children. The woman had vibrant red hair that he'd noticed the moment he'd entered. It was like a beacon—that and her laugh. He frowned. Children were dangerous in a situation such as this. They were wild cards that could become a danger to themselves and to everyone around them. Closer and to his right was another couple, Japanese; he'd heard that they were taking a vacation from their corporate jobs.

Erin looked up and smiled at him.

He smiled back and headed toward her.

"Hello," he said with what he hoped was an easygoing, guy-next-door smile. He glanced around, fidgeted and then smiled at her again. "Wow. It's a big place."

"It is," she said and put down her menu.

"I should find a seat," he said and started to turn and walk away.

C'mon, he thought, *work with me*.

Then he thought of something and turned back. "Have you been here long? I mean, have you ordered yet?" he asked, one hand on the back of the empty chair at a nearby table but his eyes were on her. He pulled out the chair and sat down at the table next to her.

"No, I haven't." Her eyes grazed over him, and she looked ready to say something before she looked away.

Instead, she leaned forward, her arms crossed and her elbows touching the table. She wasn't as thin as he'd thought. Her cleavage was deep and creamy smooth and... He drew his gaze away.

He picked up the menu and then put it down as the waiter stopped and asked what he'd like to drink. He ordered a Coke and then picked up the menu. He looked over at her. She was tapping a finger on the table.

"It's strange," he added, a note of hesitation in his voice. "I don't usually eat alone." He cleared his throat, kept his eyes on the menu even as he felt her eyes on him.

"Join me," she said.

He looked over at her, and she looked at him with a frown and less welcome in her face than her invitation justified.

"You don't mind?"

"No, of course not. I don't like eating alone. I imagine you don't, either."

"I don't." Actually, he did. He enjoyed being alone. His job demanded that he did.

"Your boyfriend's not joining you?" he asked.

"I…" She hesitated, glanced behind her and then straight at Josh.

Again he was caught, mesmerized, by the intense blue of her eyes. They were an identifying mark that pegged her immediately, a unique color that one could not fail to notice. He wondered why she hadn't obtained contacts to change the color. That fact sifted into a series of others as he noticed her hair was shorter than it had been even at the airport, shoulder length, blue black in the muted light. The wig was gone. He looked over her shoulder where a breeze seemed to move the umbrella tree whose branches hung wild and bushy near the exit. He looked away—it was nothing, no threat. He stood up and moved over to her table where he sat down across from her.

"He doesn't exist," he suggested softly as he set the menu down in front of him and looked seriously at her. He held up his hand. "I'm sorry, I didn't mean to imply…" He let the words trail off. "I just read in *Lonely Planet* of how in areas like this, young women were advised to pretend to be with a boyfriend. And I thought that maybe, that's what…"

She shook her head, looking slightly chagrined. "It's all right."

He leaned forward. "Smart move on your part." He leaned back and dropped his hands on the table, his posture open, nonthreatening. "A woman traveling alone is, especially in remote areas like this, not always wise."

"You're right and for the reason you just stated." But

even as she said it her lips thinned and she sat back, crossing her arms across her chest.

"Look, I didn't mean any offense."

"None taken. I'm on sabbatical and I've always wanted to see the caves." She shrugged, and he admired her ability to spin an off-the-cuff yarn. "None of my friends were into it, so I decided it's now or never."

"Can't say I blame you," he agreed. "I'm kind of a similar story. Just wanted a bit of adventure before winter sets in."

"Adventure," she repeated and it was as if she were turning the word over in her mind. "Yes, it is an adventure to travel to a place so remote. Most of my friends would never consider it."

"It's the perfect place." He almost grimaced at the word *perfect*. "At least from my limited experience. I'm from Coal City, Illinois. Well, that's where I grew up. You?"

"Toronto," she said softly, and he wasn't sure but he detected an edge to her voice.

"Toronto," he acknowledged. "Canada," he said with a hint of doubt in his voice. He was, after all, Josh, naive tourist, with little interest in much more than whether the Cubs would win this season and what he would choose for supper tonight on his first adventurous trip. She didn't need to know that not only did he know where Toronto was and how many miles it was from the American border, he could pinpoint every major and many minor cities in Canada and in more than a hundred other countries, as well. He also could tell her that Toronto was the fourth largest metropolis in North America and list the three that preceded it and a laundry list of those that followed.

His thoughts shifted.

Toronto.

It was brilliant. He'd thought that earlier. That the city

she'd flown out of to get to the first exit off the continent had become the one she declared as her home base. Not true, of course. He knew that she'd spent little more than the time it took to change transport before she had been on her way again.

He'd followed her trajectory from San Diego to Vancouver, Canada, where she'd arrived by bus, and then taken the train across that country before she'd taken another bus in a series of transfers out of Toronto to St. John's, Newfoundland. From there she'd taken a container ship halfway around the globe. He suspected at the time, as he still did now, that she had been making the trail as long and as distant from its source as she could. It was a logical assumption. Something an intelligent person would do, and Erin Kelley was definitely intelligent. She'd graduated high school at fifteen and a half, and finished a degree in education at nineteen. By the time she was twenty-three she had a Master's degree in education and a string of schools she'd substituted at. Fast forward six years and it brought them to this point.

"I've always wanted to go to Niagara Falls," he said. "Can't imagine what it would be like to have something like that right in the city. I imagine you'd go every day if you could."

"Not exactly in the city," she replied, and a dimple appeared in one cheek as she looked at him with an almost lighthearted look on her face.

"No?" he asked, feigning a boyish innocence combined with blatant geographical ignorance. The kind of person he deplored. "I thought it was only a taxi ride from the city center."

"Eighty miles southwest. And considering traffic around the city, well, it's not a relaxing ride. Definitely unaffordable by cab."

A crash came from the kitchen, the thud of something heavy hitting the floor. Josh schooled himself only to swing around in his chair when instinct would have had him lurching to his feet. Muffled curses and someone shouting, though he couldn't make out the words as the sound level had dropped, but they had a berating tone. Other diners were watching with animated interest to see who or what might emerge from the kitchen.

Erin was on her feet. Her face was taut, all color gone. She was closer to the edge than he had previously thought.

"Someone's supper hit the trash," the British man to their right said with a small laugh.

His gaze swept the room. Everyone else went back to their meals when nothing else happened. Josh kept one eye on Erin and one on the kitchen. He saw the back of the chef and the raised arms. Erin looked stricken, as if she would bolt at any second. He had to treat this seriously, secure the area, a big step in the trajectory of their relationship and gaining the trust he needed.

He placed his hand over hers. "Calamity in the kitchen," he said. "I'll go check. I paid my dues in a commercial kitchen as a teenager."

As he stood, he noticed her knuckles were white and he suspected that she didn't realize how tightly her hands gripped the edge of the table.

Relief seemed to flood her face even as her gaze flicked to the exit. She was staying on top of things. *Good girl,* he thought. *Keep your eyes on the exit at all times. But don't bolt—not yet.*

"It's nothing, I'm sure," he said. This was the first chance he'd had to place the thought in her head that he could protect her.

It was a big break and a big first step to being Erin Argon's boyfriend and getting her the hell out of here before everything broke loose.

Chapter Nine

Erin took a deep breath.

The only thing pinning her to the chair was the unwanted attention continuing to stand would draw to herself and, oddly, Josh's calm reaction. She'd pushed her chair slightly at an angle so she could see both the kitchen and the exit and took a series of deep breaths.

A string of words, what sounded from their inflection like curses of some kind, emanated from the kitchen. As the closest table to the kitchen, she got the benefit of the amplified kitchen noise. The rest of the diners had already lost interest. She leaned on her arms, her hands grasping her elbows, in an attempt to control her chattering nerves. She watched as the chef excitedly waved a wooden spoon and a smaller man said something that was so toned down as to be equally as incomprehensible. Her gaze shifted to Josh, who was in the middle saying something. But now it was difficult to hear. The only thing she knew for sure was that they weren't speaking English. And she only knew that from catching the odd word. Words she didn't understand.

She wondered how he knew what was being said and then realized he probably didn't. But it didn't matter. His manner was what was getting their attention. She'd noticed that about him, his calm presence that under normal circumstances she would have instinctively trusted. Except she'd learned over these past months to trust no one but Mike, who was now out of contact. She was on her own.

He shrugged as he came back. "Someone's dinner is going to be a little late. Steak burned. And the rest…" He shrugged. "On the floor."

"That's it?" she asked and was relieved that the tremor that had shot through her body since the first inkling of trouble was now silent.

"That's it," he agreed as he sat down. "Bit of competition between the chef and his help." Josh laughed. "Worse, he's from the Czech Republic and when he gets excited he reverts to his native tongue. I had to jump in, as all anyone understood was anger. Once I got through to him that he'd flipped languages and no one understood him…" He shrugged. "He switched to English and everything was good."

"You spoke to him in Czech? Is that what you're saying?" Surprise ran through her. It wasn't a common second language, at least not where she was from. "And you know that how?"

"Born there," he said easily. "First generation Czech, too young to remember the place, though. Folks left before I was even talking."

She hadn't expected that. Josh seemed solid, made at home geek, born in America. Now he was telling her he had a bit of an exotic past. Dark hair curled around his ears, and somehow she hadn't noticed the chiseled planes in his face or the sharp intelligence in his eyes. There had been so much about him that had been hidden by the ball cap and the dark, slightly unflattering glasses. Her heart raced momentarily considering what else she might have missed—who he was and his threat potential. She met his eyes head-on.

"You never went back?"

He shrugged. "Once. It's a long story and the history of the region is boring dinner talk."

"So you grew up in the United States, but…" She couldn't help staring at the new Josh. She looked away.

"But I speak Czech," he said easily. "You know how it is when your parents are from somewhere else." He laughed. "No, I suppose you don't." He shrugged. "They spoke Czech at home, to each other, so I got a pretty good handle on the language."

"Oh," she said. Darkness had settled around them. It seemed to draw long fingers into the room, meshing on the edges of the light, threatening to take over. She gave herself a small shake. Her imagination was in overdrive again.

But she couldn't seem to help it. She hated this time of day. It made her feel vulnerable somehow. Yet despite the jarring incident in the kitchen, the darkness and this morning's tragedy, she felt calmer than she'd felt all day.

He picked up the menu, held it for a minute as if he wanted to say something. His thumb tapped against the glossy cardboard, his fingernail white and well-manicured.

She supposed that went along with who he was, a citified man. A man whose closest brush with nature would be the boardwalk leading to the caves.

He opened the menu and glanced briefly over the top of it. "I'm not sure what to choose."

Her menu lay in front of her. She picked it up and opened it, glancing through the choices.

"The problem is I like everything that's on here." He lowered the menu and smiled at her.

She couldn't help but offer him a tentative smile back.

There was so little that was threatening about him, and she'd already deemed him a nonthreat, she reminded herself. She wouldn't be sitting here with him otherwise. And more than likely, considering who was after her, he would have liquefied her by now if that had been his plan. She shuddered. *Liquefy.* It was an outrageous word, a movie word—nothing more.

"Are you cold?"

"No, I'm fine. Thanks." She lowered the menu and looked at him, surprised for a moment at the knowing that lurked deep in his brown eyes. And just as quickly, that sense of knowledge was gone and his eyes hid nothing more intense than the smile he offered her.

Keep your distance.

"What made you come to Malaysia?" He set down the menu. "I mean alone. That must have been difficult."

You have no idea.

She'd hated being alone, and in Singapore she'd stumbled on a woman who had briefly become a friend: Emma. She'd enjoyed Emma's company in the short time she had been there and had been grateful for a place to stay. But when she'd left, she'd disappeared, leaving only a brief note. Nothing online, nothing traceable. She'd followed that rule, Mike's rule, to the letter. Georgetown was where she'd made her mistake. Tears pricked the backs of her eyes, and she willed them away with a mental effort that she'd honed these past months. Tears were counterproductive, and she hadn't cried since she'd crossed the US border, possibly for the last time. The back of her neck felt hot and her stomach tightened. She took a breath and fought for the feeling of normalcy, for the ability to project the illusion. This time, getting close would only be an illusion and she'd pull away before anything could happen. She wouldn't make that mistake again.

"I'm sorry," he said. "I've made you uncomfortable."

"No, it's all right. I've just had some bad news."

"Anything I can do?"

"No." She shook her head. "Nothing that won't re-solve itself."

"Good then," he said. "Man, I'm starved. Did you notice the special of the day? It might be a better alternative than this darn menu." He shook his head. "Never give a hungry man too many choices, not when they all look good."

"No, I…" She shook her head, relieved to change the subject. She hadn't really looked at the menu. She'd lifted it up, held it in front of her for enough minutes to have read it, but the truth was that she hadn't even given a thought to it. Less than eight hours ago a man had died in an explosion meant for her. She couldn't focus, couldn't get it out of her mind. She blinked. She had to stop thinking about it. Forward was the only option. "I'm not particularly hungry."

"Pizza," he said with a smile.

She drew in a quiet breath and smiled.

"Would you like to share the standard, pepperoni, Italian sausage—"

"Mushrooms," she finished and laughed. She hoped the laugh had sounded natural. But then she was hyper-critical of her acting ability, knowing what failure to put on a good act could mean.

"Mushrooms," he agreed. "Goes without saying. You're in?"

"Definitely. I'll share, but nothing large unless you're hungry."

"And a small salad," he added.

She nodded gratefully. She hadn't had pizza in months. Not that it hadn't been available, but she hadn't done more than go to school and return to her small apartment to eat and sleep before starting the routine again the next day.

She'd stayed low, stayed off the streets. That was until just a week ago when she'd begun to go out a little, lead a normal life, think the heat was off.

She'd been mistaken.

She looked up and met his straightforward, almost honest gaze. He was exactly as she'd originally judged him to be—safe. There didn't seem to be anything nefarious or dangerous about him.

She toyed with her napkin and then dropped it. She needed to take charge, take the lead.

"Have you booked any tours?" she asked as she set her menu aside. But before he could answer, the waiter was at their table requesting their orders.

"Medium pizza." Josh listed the ingredients. "And a Greek salad." Josh smiled at her. "Greek is good?"

"Of course," she said with more cheer in her voice than she was feeling. "How did you know?" The words slipped out. She drew in a breath. That was unacceptable and could lead to mistakes.

"Know what?"

"Which salad I like." She shook her head, giving herself a mental shake, as well. "Of course you didn't. That was a ridiculous thing to say."

"I'm sorry, I should have asked." Josh's lips pressed together and he cracked his knuckles as if overcome by a case of nerves.

"It's all right. No worries, really."

"Doesn't everyone like Greek?" Josh asked and there was a look of puzzlement on his face.

Geeky and safe, she thought with not so much emphasis on the first as there had been when she'd first seen him.

Instead, the word *safe* seemed to ring in her mind, and for once in her long flight she had the odd sense of coming home.

DESPITE WHAT JOSH thought of the actions that had brought Erin to this place, there was something that drew her to him. Maybe it was the self-deprecating smile on her face that he found sexy or her lips that were full and beautifully kissable.

He shouldn't be thinking about her like that, like anything but an assignment. But it had been a long time since he'd been in a relationship that was anything but a one-night stand. This assignment had ridden tight on the back of another that had taken him through central Europe. There had been no thought or time for women or clandestine affairs. There was no time for such now.

A look behind him confirmed that the older couple to their left and one table behind were finishing their dessert. The accent in their voices, mannerisms and the bits of conversation he caught indicated that they came from northern England. The man had a pallid look to him but a strong jaw line that spoke of someone who could be relied on in a pinch. He watched as they spoke and how they gestured. Married, he guessed with accuracy that rarely failed. Longstanding, he also suspected from the way they sat in long, easy moments of silence. To his right, two men were focused only on each other, and as he watched, one's hand covered the others. They had been the ones with the ultra-conservative luggage and now their conversation was intense, every look, every movement, focused on each other. He'd ruled them out earlier as no threat.

"Were you planning to go to the caves tomorrow?" he asked, turning his attention back to her.

"I suppose," she said. "No." She shook her head with a smile. "Definitely. Why else would I be here? I'm sorry. I was distracted." She threaded the fingers of one hand through those of the other.

You're not too sure about any trip, because that's not why you're here.

Her thinly arched brows met slightly closer together as she turned her attention back to him. The eyebrows were only part of her disguise but an effective part. Past girlfriends and keen observation had him recognizing a cosmetically altered brow. It was an obvious attempt to make the natural arch of her brows into something else.

She leaned forward, her body language encouraging him, and he knew immediately that her thoughts were aligning with his. She was setting him up to be the temporary boyfriend, the smokescreen, taking her out of the role of single woman traveling alone. It was all becoming too easy. Of course, this could all be the proverbial calm before the storm.

"Shall we?" he asked as he slid the payment folder to the center of the table.

"I really wish you'd let me…"

"Gentleman's prerogative," he said with a slightly suggestive smile.

Ten minutes later they were at her door. He bent down, meaning to give her a friendly kiss on the cheek. Instead, she put her hands lightly on his shoulders and turned her head, kissing him full on the lips—a closed-mouth kiss but a kiss just the same.

"Good night, Josh," she whispered as she turned and unlocked the door.

Bravo, he thought. She'd taken charge of the situation, stepped in and made the first move, placing him in position to be the boyfriend she needed. It was a brilliant strategy and damn fine work for an amateur. And he tried not to think of how much willpower it had taken not to do more than just kiss her. He had been tempted like he hadn't in a very long time. He imagined what she would taste like, what her curves would feel like against him instead of the teasing brush that had been reality.

Instead, he continued to pretend he was a naive tourist and whispered, "Good night," before turning and heading back the way they had come.

Chapter Ten

The rock gleamed, stark and impenetrable by the light of Josh's flashlight. It was just before midnight and his watch alarm would rouse him to announce the beginning of a new day in less than five hours.

For a second he took in the caves through the eyes of a tourist. Clearwater Cave, at over one hundred miles in explored length, was once thought to be the longest cave in the world. The sheer grandeur of nature's beauty carved in rock was awe inspiring even at midnight by the light of a flashlight. But natural beauty and inspiration were not what he was looking for.

"I hope to hell this is all redundant information," he muttered. So far he'd marked off the pathway, checked out both Deer and Wind Caves with the intent of ending this night's tour here, at the one cave that could circumvent trouble better than either the walkway—too visible—or the jungle—too impenetrable.

The mouth of Clearwater Cave loomed large, a hollowed black monolith that was intimidating by the light of day, never mind against the backdrop of the night sky. The system went on for miles with individual caves linking up to others giving the illusion of a singular cave. While he'd been here before on another assignment more than four years ago, he had only explored these caves virtually.

The assignment had been over within hours, the targets easily disposed of.

The light grazed the rough rock, gray-brown and dense with the wear of time. Like the two caves that had come before, this one had walkways that made it easy for the amateur to explore with the added safety of a guide. What would make escape more difficult were all the places off the walkway, the nooks and crannies that could hide a killer.

In other circumstances he would be impressed by the magnitude of it all. The cave was as massive and awe in-spiring as the brochure had promised. He shone his flash-light into the dark depths, but the light couldn't touch the outer reaches of the cave. It was that large. He returned the light to the walkway. He skimmed a hand along the rail that kept the tourists safely away from the vast middle of the cave where rough rock outcroppings and stalagmites made exploration treacherous.

A snake slithered along the railing. The flood of light had disturbed its nighttime hunt, and its slim length gleamed an eerie blue black in the artificial light. Josh pushed forward, ignoring the cave-racer snake, a nonpoi-sonous variety that fed mostly on bats. The information rattled through his mind even as he passed the reptile. The only snakes he was interested in were those of the warm-blooded variety.

His flashlight skirted over the walls where insects crawled through crevices. Other creatures hid there, as well, but nowhere that his light hit was there a crevice large enough to hide a man. The light swept the walkway and across into the main part of the cave where stalag-mites and craters peppered the cave floor, which was slick with bat guano. It was there where the danger would hide, and it was also there where they could escape if need be.

He needed a handle on all exit points no matter how difficult an exit it might prove. The only thing he didn't plan to check was walking out. For that would involve getting through thick jungle and climbing limestone cliffs. It was an arduous trip that only the fittest would attempt. It wasn't an option easily scouted, and it wasn't one he planned to take, not with a woman who had no experience rock climbing.

He bent down, grabbed the top of the railing and swung over. He landed with a small thump on the soft mat of the cave floor. The light continued to skim over time-smoothed rock, musty with the damp that had settled like a second skin. The dank blackness thickened and surrounded him as he stepped tentatively along the slick floor, the bat guano feet deep in places.

At the back of this cave was a river, one he hadn't needed to check out on the one previous visit, for that had been a different kind of assignment. The river was part of a convoluted underground water system that was thought to have created the caves. More important, it was a probable escape hatch. One he hoped they wouldn't need.

Ahead there was a deeper, impenetrable blackness, one that wasn't touched by the moonlit-streaked night that was faltering the farther he was from the entrance. The darkness seemed to draw tight around him, the silence continually broken by the squeaks of thousands of bats.

He slipped and caught his balance. The light shifted wildly, skirting across the rock.

"Damn it," he muttered through clenched teeth. He could easily lose his balance, slide and fall into what was basically a giant bat toilet. The smell, considering it all, wasn't bad. Instead, it was a dank, rich, slightly fetid scent. He'd smelled worse on other assignments in other places. Much worse. And for a second he remembered the spoils of war, and the horror of rotting corpses in the midst of insurgencies in poverty-ridden countries.

"Fifty," he muttered, counting off his steps. Each was approximately a two-foot advance into the cave. According to the map, the first access to the underground river would be a matter of following the wooden walkway along the perimeter of the cave.

He stopped and switched off the light. There was a different sound now, a feeling to the vast emptiness that hadn't been there before. He switched on the light and peered into the blackness. There was nothing beyond where the sliver of light from the flashlight splashed. He turned around. The entrance was more than one hundred feet back, where the last of the evening light had vanished. There the moon shone down and provided some light, some reprieve. The darkness, the hollow rock that held so much unseen life, all of it was a challenge that ran a sliver of fear along his backbone and made his whole being come alive.

"Sixty-three." He counted off his steps under his breath, his attention focused again on the immediate surroundings. The cave was off-limits this late at night. Tourists were to keep away from the caves at these hours. They were dangerous, and they'd all been given a copy of the rules, printed in tourist pamphlets and reiterated by resort staff. It had been clear from the beginning. People had died in these caves by not following the rules. It was the standard mantra, and it worked. The mass of people believed and followed rules, fearful of the consequences of noncompliance. It wasn't that people hadn't died, but the dangers were not as excessive or as common as tourists were led to believe. But it worked for the majority. Traveling in safe groups and staying at a safe resort was enough adventure for the average city dweller.

The darkness was changing slightly. There was a different feel to it. The light shone on what appeared to be a dip and a narrowing of the walls and an increased feel of dampness in the air.

He continued to count off his steps as the light skittered over a rock ledge that smoothed out into an odd-looking beach, minus the sand. Around him was the chilly dampness of a place that never saw the sun. Ahead of him was a calm, but he suspected deceptive, band of water. The river ran underground through much of this cave, except here where it opened up, skirting rock and eventually leading to the outside. Here, no bats shifted in the dark, only other creatures of the night, rats and other rodents, snakes and the insects that made their home along the rock banks of this strange cave river—all of them, for now, harmless.

The flashlight was waterproof, as was the knapsack on his back. He clipped the flashlight to a reinforced rope that hung around his neck, peeled off his jacket followed by his shirt and put them both into his knapsack. He hadn't been much of a swimmer until he'd joined the CIA and become a field agent; then it had become a necessary skill. He took a deep breath and cracked his knuckles.

One foot slipped into the water as his hand touched the ledge, and he took a deep breath before dropping into the river without another thought. Research had given him all the information he needed. The water closed around him and for a second a tremor of warning ran through him, for it felt like a trap.

He treaded water before taking a breath and heading into the murky unknown with long, powerful strokes. The water was invigorating, not chilly but not warm, either. He dived under, circumventing the rock that skimmed across the first stretch of the river and came up for breath ten feet away where the rock peeled back and only bracketed the sides of the river, closing in on either side, darker than the night that surrounded it, more ominous. For it was there that he could see the occasional gleam of the nocturnal cave dwellers' eyes as they watched and somehow seemed to monitor his progress.

The air changed as the river exited from the dank confines of the cave. It was a river where guides brought the more adventurous tourists to swim. A thrill he suspected for some. Water dripped from his hair and he shook his head, scattering droplets around him. He boosted himself over the ledge and stood up. It hadn't been an arduous swim, not for him. But the question was, could she do it? What he'd learned of her was that she'd had swimming lessons as a child, nothing much past beginner classes but enough to know the basics. So what kind of swimmer was she? He could take her clinging to his back if necessary, but would it be necessary?

He glanced at his watch—12:40 a.m.

His arm scraped against an outcropping of limestone. Water dripped into his eyes, and he pushed his hair back with splayed fingers. There was no indication of danger yet, but time was running out. Two special agents had arranged to meet them in Georgetown, and from there they would get her back to the States and placed in the witness protection program, leaving him to deal with the Anarchists' man or men, as it might be.

It was a good plan as such plans went, still untried and subject to variables they had yet to anticipate.

The evening air basked warmly around him, and he knew he'd be dry in minutes. And as he began the walk back to the resort, his thoughts were on Erin and the most difficult part of his assignment still ahead. There was little time and because of that a premium on establishing trust.

Chapter Eleven

"Thirty," Erin muttered through clenched teeth as she powered through another push-up. Full push-up, no woman's version. She'd graduated into the real thing over two months ago. Push-ups, sit-ups, running in place—now it was all part of her daily regimen.

The sun streaked through the window, the early morning rays already heating the little room as the fan twirled overhead. She thought about turning on the air conditioner as she stood up and looked at her watch: 5:30 a.m.

"You'd be an hour from getting up in the old days," she said and shook her head. "Talking to myself. When will that ever end?"

She turned her mind off distracting thoughts and instead concentrated on fifteen minutes of jogging in place.

Twenty minutes later she was untying her ponytail and reaching for the shower knob.

"Japan," she murmured. "That's far enough away." She put her hand under the water, checking the temperature. "Train for part of the way, maybe through Bangkok." She stepped into the shower. "English as a second language. Emma said everyone was doing it there, in Japan. I'd blend into a sea of Westerners." She grabbed the soap and hummed a tuneless verse, made up for all she knew. It didn't belong to a song she could think of.

Water sluiced down her body as she soaped and lathered and absently noticed how her curves were less full, firmer. Her soft, desk-formed body had transformed into an athlete's body, and despite the fact that it had been of necessity she was beginning to appreciate it.

She reached down and turned off the water.

"You have to stay focused," she reminded herself.

A bird whistled outside and then followed with a strange warble and the gecko that seemed to reside in her room continued its cricket-like chirp. Otherwise everything was quiet.

She looked out the window where she could see dense jungle on the other side of the walkway. With a second-from-the-end room, and the room beside her newly vacated, she had a privacy that the others did not. It was something she suspected could be advantageous to someone in her situation. She could easily run, hide in the jungle.

Dressed, she grabbed her bag and opened the door even as she took a deep, troubled breath. Leaves rustled and the S-path of a lizard imprinted on the thick foliage beneath the wooden walkway. Erin shivered. She disliked reptiles of any kind.

Soon she was in the hotel gift shop and five minutes later, she fingered a map she'd purchased there. It was a fairly decent map. If nothing else it showed the proximity of the Mulu caves in relation to the rest of Malaysia.

"Don't go anywhere without a back door, a way out." She whispered the words that Mike had emphasized again and again during the flurry of activity that had led to her flight. Thoughts of home and family overwhelmed her. She would be an aunt by now if Sarah had had the baby.

She pushed thoughts of home from her mind. Home distracted her and took her out of the moment. She became less observant and more vulnerable as a result. She'd learned that on a train through the Black Sea region in Russia when her pouch had almost gone missing. She'd closed her eyes at the wrong moment, drifted into a catnap with thoughts of home lulling her and only by chance had she awoken in time to stop the man attempting to cut her pouch free from her waist with a knife. She'd screamed and for the first time on her flight, drawn attention to herself. It was enough to have the man slink back to his seat as if nothing had happened. She'd huddled in hers and exited immediately at the next stop. Since then, she'd beefed up security on the pouch that carried everything of importance. A wire cord that couldn't be easily cut had replaced the leather one, and the pouch itself was now out of view, under her clothes.

"Erin!"

She turned as Josh flagged her down with a one-armed wave.

"You're a long way away. Daydreaming?" His voice had a teasing note.

"No, I'm fine. I was just…" Her fingers trembled. *Damn it*, she thought. *Get it together.*

"Erin?" He moved closer, and the faint scent of pine that might be shaving gel and fresh air wafted around her. She noticed the definition of his upper arm, like that of a man who worked out—one who was fit. She frowned but didn't move away.

"What's wrong?"

She tried to smile. "Nothing…"

Everything. I'm running. I'm alone and I'm terrified for my family, for myself.

The thoughts ran through her mind even as she wrestled them into submission.

"You're sure?" Concern played across his face.

"Yes. Just feeling a little down."

"Classic single traveler syndrome. Being alone, I mean. It can bum you out." His voice was low and smooth, self-assured like it hadn't been before.

Her palms were slick with sweat from the heat and something else that she refused to give credence to. She moved away, disconcerted. Everything about him was tough and toned. And all of that brought her up short.

His eyes were a cinnamon color and she was drawn to them like this was the first time she'd seen them. The sunlight glinted on a steel stud in his left ear.

Who was Josh Sedovich?

"Josh?" His name was tentative on her lips. He wasn't the geek he'd presented himself to be, that much was becoming clear. Or was it? Had her imagination just gone into overdrive? She'd had moments of this throughout the past five months. It was suspicion where in the end no suspicion was warranted. But it was better than the alternative—what had happened in Georgetown could never happen again. No one else must die because of her.

She clenched her fists, her nails digging deep. This was so hard. That was why in Georgetown it had been such a relief to strike up casual friendships.

Daniel.

"It wasn't your fault."

"What?" *What the heck? Was he reading her mind?*

"Whatever it is that's bothering you. It's not your fault."

She bit back a sigh of relief. Except that soon it would be common knowledge. Especially now that she had disappeared. Only she hadn't. She was registered under the name she'd used in Georgetown. She needed a new alias and she needed it soon.

Local teacher's car explodes.

The headline was as clear in her mind as if he had said it or as if the news line had flashed before her eyes. Her heart raced and she had to quell the urge to bolt.

Three days. It seemed like forever, and she could only hope that it was soon enough.

"So what do you do when you're not vacationing?" Erin asked that afternoon.

Josh looked at the worn tips of his hiking boots, boots that had seen many mountains. He'd hiked mountain trails and rock climbed and on one assignment he'd even parachuted from a plane. It was all part of the job.

"Civic administrator," he replied. It was a fairly dull career that no one tended to ask further questions about. "You?"

"I teach," she said as if that general term covered it all.

"If I were to guess I'd say grade school," he said with a smile. "You look like you'd be good with kids."

She looked at him, startled, and he wondered if he had pushed her too hard.

"Just a guess." He shrugged.

"You're right," she said softly. There was a note of pride in her voice. "I love kids," she said. "It's why I chose grade school education." She hesitated.

He smiled. It was an easy conversation that surprised him, as it had been unplanned. "The only kids I know are those of a good friend of mine. Suzette calls me the drop-in, spoil-them-to-death uncle." He shrugged. "They call me uncle even though I'm not."

"Sounds like you enjoy them."

"I do but I don't get them. Don't see enough kids, I

guess, to be able to relate. But they do seem to love me, at least from the way they scream and jump all over me when I arrive." He shrugged. "Could be the gifts I bring."

"I've always loved kids," Erin said softly.

"Is that regret I hear?"

"No, I... No, not really."

He sat down on the edge of a lounge chair. "What brought you here?"

"Teaching English as a second language," she said without hesitation. "I began the whole journey because of that and then unexpectedly got an opportunity to teach at a private primary school. It was a temporary fill-in." There was a tight set to her mouth and a sorrowful look in her eyes.

"So, planning to go home?"

Her lips tightened and pain seemed to dance briefly in her eyes before she met his with a dazzling smile. "I may travel for a bit first."

His eyes locked with hers. The startling sapphire blue held a hint of smoky mystery that hadn't been there before. He dropped his gaze and wished he hadn't stopped at the milky white skin where one collarbone pushed up against the delicate film of her blouse, and the rise of her breasts forced him to look away.

"Josh? I'm curious—the earring. Why the ace of spades?"

"A reminder," he said shortly, more shortly than he'd intended.

"Really," she said. "The ace of spades—the highest card in the deck and the death card. Interesting choice."

The highest card always wins, he thought. *Even over death.*

She smiled at him and placed a hand on his wrist. The touch was featherlight, and for a minute it was as if there was nothing else, only the two of them.

"I'm planning to go to Deer Cave and see the bats. Leaving at four. I imagine that will be enough time. I want to enjoy the hike, stop, take some pictures."

It took him a second to realize what she had said. His senses were still so full of her touch, her nearness.

She stood up.

"Alone?" *Not in this lifetime*, he thought grimly. He glanced at his watch. Sid Mylo had outsourced as he'd thought he would. Tenuk had just confirmed that at least one man in addition to Bobbie had arrived in Asia via Hong Kong. There was no word on Sid, and that was what worried him. They were still safe despite being stuck here longer than he'd planned. Tenuk had watches posted. Still, he wasn't taking a chance. She wouldn't be alone. Not that there wouldn't be other tourists. Strangers. It wouldn't happen. He was on her like glue.

"Want to come along?"

"I'd love to." He inwardly cringed at the use of the word *love*. It was not a word, except in the context of a relationship with a woman, that he would use to describe anything. It was a girly word that didn't fit into his world, but it fitted his current persona. He stood up. He admired the casual way in which she had thrown out the invitation. She was not as street blind as he had thought, but not nearly street savvy enough. At least her asking had saved him manipulating the invitation.

She rubbed her bottom lip with her tongue, an endearing habit that he noticed she did when she was out of her element. A habit that was not something forced or put on, and not something a professional should ever do. But she wasn't a professional.

For a moment, as the silence shrouded them, the jungle seemed to close in around them.

"I'll meet you here." She lifted her wrist and looked at

her watch. "In, say, an hour? I'd like to leave early, well before four even, take my time along the walk."

"Sounds good. Do you have a map?" The question was redundant—he had mapped and tracked the area, and the layout was clear in his mind, not to mention the walkway that was impossible to get lost on.

"Yes," she said. "No worries. I'm good with a map."

"Well, at least someone is," he said in his best Josh the Geek voice.

He watched her leave with a slight swing of her hips and realized for the first time that when this assignment was over he wasn't so sure he could just walk away without a second thought.

"Get it together, Sedovich," he muttered as the revolver tucked in the waistband of his pants pressed against his back, and his mind began to go over the intricate layout of the cave that contained the intriguing underground river.

His gaze followed her even as he made sure she wasn't aware of his vigilance. But the truth was that he wouldn't let her out of his sight.

Chapter Twelve

"This is amazing," Erin said as she snapped a picture an hour and a half later. "Josh?" She looked at him with a slight frown. "Can you believe this? Look." Her finger brushed along the wooden rail on the walkway within inches of a stick insect—its long, wood-like body was motionless as it seemed poised to wait and see what they might do next. She slipped a small disposable camera from her pocket and took a picture.

Fine lines bracketed her mouth. They hadn't been there in the pictures he had seen of her before her flight.

He pulled his gaze to her eyes where interest and something else sparked. They both knew what the something else was—fear, anxiety, the threat of death that haunted her.

"It is," he agreed and shadowed her as he pulled out the cheap camera he'd purchased in a market in Singapore.

"Special forces took out a man in Kuala Lumpur," Tenuk *said as the morning sun cast a glare from behind.*

"Dead?"

"Unfortunately," Tenuk said. "No answers from a corpse and no word who or what might be following him."

"Too close. I need to get her out of here. I've got to get hold of Wade."

"That might be exactly what they expect. Sit tight. Let's keep to the original plan for now."

He shook his head. The conversation with Tenuk had only been this morning. He had rethought logistics but found Tenuk was right. The Malaysian Special Forces kill had taken the assassins back a step. He turned his attention to Erin and hurried to join her, but she was already heading up the walkway as if the Mulu bat cave was the most important tourist attraction that she would ever see.

"Hey, stop for a minute." He puffed as if the ten minutes of easy walking combined with an additional twenty minutes of power walking had exhausted him. "Slow down."

She stopped and turned around, one hand on her hip. But as their eyes met she looked suddenly confused, as though she wasn't sure who he was.

"Slow down?" She took a step toward him. "You're not out of breath. In fact, you don't sound strained at all despite the heat." She backtracked another few steps. "You must work out."

"I do." He hesitated. "When I have the chance."

"I suppose that explains it." But there was doubt in her voice as she wiped the sheen of sweat from her forehead.

He shrugged. "I've started running." Actually, he trained in heat—ran marathons in weather almost as hot as this. And hours at the gym made the mile they'd gone in ninety-degree heat nothing. He should have dabbed a bit of water from his water bottle on his forehead, given the illusion of sweat. It was a glaring error.

Damn, he thought. He'd been distracted. She'd distracted him. That had never happened before, and it couldn't happen now. But the line between feigning interest and having an interest seemed to be thinning despite his efforts.

They took their time for the next stretch of the walkway. It was an easy walk, the earlier power walking unnecessary considering how much time she'd allowed. She had been pushing his limits, testing him, he suspected. And again, that had surprised him. There was more to her, more layers than he had expected.

And as he thought that she turned around, fixing him with those blue eyes of hers that made him think of other things, things that had no place between them.

"I don't think it's that much farther."

In fact, it wasn't. It was fifty yards straight ahead. It had been dark last night, but that and past experience told him everything he needed to know. There was a path in and out, but they could go farther if necessary, to another cave where their options of getting out increased in the form of the underground cavern he'd explored only last night. Not the best option but an exit strategy should it be needed.

"You're sure?" he asked as if none of those thoughts ran through his mind.

She waved a map, the typical over-glossed, underdetailed resort pamphlet.

"Erin."

"What?" She swung around to look at him.

She smiled in a way that in another life would have drawn him. He would have been all over getting to know her. But here the game they played was much more complicated.

His fingers brushed her shoulder and for a moment it felt as though the world stopped as electricity seemed to dance between them. She shivered beneath his touch, turning to face him, almost in slow motion. He ached to hold her, but a movement just over her left shoulder took that ache away. For a moment his breath stopped and his whole being stilled.

Silence beat between them as the plush rise of her breast pressed against his arm. He was aware of it like he was so many other details, but his full attention was focused on labeling the movement as danger or...

He drew in a quiet breath and pointed to his left, in the direction where the flattened grass in the shape of an S indicated the predator was nonhuman. It was a lizard.

They continued along the wooden walk. His senses were now in overdrive. The dense foliage was problematic, but he'd known that going in. The air was humid, thick like the plant-choked jungle that seemed to reach and tantalize and even tease. Anything could hide in there as the lizard had already proven.

Beneath the walkway was a land mine of natural threats. The giant lizards that weaved easily through the long grass, the insects that were oversized and loud and screeched from their green sanctuary while humans were confined to the resort's boardwalks for their own safety, he suspected, more than for the protection of the environment. He felt rather like an animal in a cage, except he was free to escape the boundaries of the wooden railing at any time and at his own peril.

He peered over the railing. The ground was more than ten feet down and lush with tall grass. When he tilted his head and looked up, vines wound around the trees, a green labyrinth of plant life. The jungle provided a screen, a screen that he didn't like.

He hurried to close the distance between them as she made her way determinedly along the path. And he thought again of how easily she became a tourist rather than a woman on the run. There had been only amateur acting in the background he'd been briefed on, yet she appeared to be acting very well.

As if to dispute that thought, she turned around and there was a look of panic in her eyes. "I've got to go back."

"Back?" He was puzzled. "But we're almost there."

"Claustrophobia," she said as she pushed past him. "I… The thought of a tight, enclosed space…" Her hands clenched, and he could see her knuckles were white. "I thought I could do this. It was so long ago when I planned this trip."

Claustrophobia? He questioned that immediately. Her voice sounded strained but not panicked, not the terror of a phobia. There had been no mention of that in any of the comprehensive research he'd received.

"Claustrophobia?" he repeated. "You're sure?"

"I… I just can't do it, Josh."

It didn't fit her profile, not the textbook version or the real. For the space of a few seconds he was stumped, and then realized what it was: loss of control—an environment that she couldn't choreograph.

"Excuse, excuse." A small man came up to them, his companion a few feet away. They'd been walking at a leisurely pace but now they were walking fast; he'd been monitoring their progress since he'd first become aware of them more than ten minutes ago. It had taken them that long to catch up.

He gritted his teeth. "Yes?" he asked with forced politeness.

"Can you read this, please?" The man held out a brochure similar to the one Erin carried.

No threat. He'd determined that hours ago, since their arrival. They'd arrived on the flight after theirs. They were a couple, five years married, celebrating an anniversary before returning to corporate jobs in Tokyo. The only issue was that they were tourists whose first language was Japanese. It had been Tenuk who had gotten that bit of information. Between the two of them they were cobbling together a profile on each of the guests.

He looked at the pamphlet they were holding.

"I speak English," the man explained. "Reading, not as well."

"What do you need?"

"When does Deer Cave close?"

Josh glanced through the pamphlet and immediately saw the problem. Despite a long and drawn out history and current facts, there were no times of viewing. It was obviously a printing screwup that the resort had failed to catch.

"The tours have stopped for today. We're on our own." He smiled at them. "The best show is still to come. The bats will emerge just before dusk." He glanced at the sky, saw that the sun had shifted and settled lower. "You can follow us if you'd like."

"Thank you," the man said solemnly. The woman again said nothing. Instead, she nervously bit her nails and stood in the shadows just behind the man's right shoulder. She seemed rather timid as if…

He watched the man put a hand on the nervous woman's arm, giving her a silent message, a warning maybe. Josh felt his whole body tense, prepared to defend, to interject. He watched for the woman's reaction.

Any sign of fear in her demeanor and he was prepared to jump in. His eyes met the woman's. Here was the moment of truth. Her gaze was soulful, her eyes a deep rich brown that held no fear and no hurt. Instead, she smiled, one that was tentative but not trembling.

She put her hand in the crook of the man's arm.

Josh blew out a breath. If there was one thing that could send him off the straight trajectory of a mission, it was a woman who wasn't being treated well. He had been raised by a mother who had fled that kind of abuse. At the time he'd been too young to do anything. But when he was older, he'd paid his father a visit and let him know exactly what he thought of him. While there'd been nothing physical, the last words he'd left his father had, in a way, been like blows.

His hand slipped into his pocket. He fingered the worn beads, a single earring, not even a pair. That was all he had left to remind him of the fragility of life.

"Josh?"

He swung around to find Erin beside him. He'd taken his eyes off her—lost track of her position. He blinked to clear his mind.

There was still panic in her eyes but it was muted by a look of determination that was accented in the thin line of her usually full lips. "I'm sorry. That was silly of me. I do want to see the bats. And the cave, too, but I suppose that will be tomorrow as tours are done for the day." The tremor in her voice wasn't put on.

He put a hand on her waist, half expecting her to brush it off. She didn't, and something felt right about his hand being there. They barely knew each other, were little more than strangers, yet they needed to be so much more. His touch moved from a light brushing of his fingers to something more solid. He could feel her firm, warm flesh beneath the thin blouse, the well-toned and slim lines that held not an inch of extra flesh, evidence of the physical toning she had done in these months of flight.

"Let's do this," she said. She moved a few inches away, and he was forced to drop his hand.

Behind them the couple spoke in excited undertones as they hurried behind them, and they all walked at a fast pace. They had ten minutes to make the final quarter mile hike to the observatory.

He adjusted his ball cap and took the rear.

Chapter Thirteen

This wasn't a good idea, Erin thought. Dusk was approaching and they were heading deeper into the jungle. It didn't matter that it was a quite civilized, wide wooden plank walkway that kept them away from the jungle's depths. It was still a place that was foreign, unknown. If anyone was following her, if someone had landed at the resort, then she was here, trapped.

Trapped.

What had compelled her to take this hike knowing the possibilities of what might happen? Whoever was after her would know by now that she hadn't died in the car explosion in Georgetown. Whoever was following her more than likely knew who had died and who she was.

How soon would they come after her?

It came to her as she fought off the tendrils of panic, that the jungle and the approaching dark provided cover both for the hunter and the hunted.

Where had she read that?

It didn't matter.

She glanced at Josh. She liked him. In another time or place he would be a friend. But that wasn't what surprised her. What surprised her was that she found herself attracted to him. That was an emotion that in her current circumstance she had no time for and one she had to ignore.

Despite feelings of friendship or the desire to get close, if the worst happened, she reminded herself she needed to run and not consider the rest, the others on this trail. She had to remember Sarah and what would happen if they knew what her sister had seen.

But there were others and she would endanger them.

She'd run. That thought played over and over in her mind.

But in Georgetown there'd been no choice, no survivors, no one to save.

Tears threatened, and she struggled to hold them off. Daniel.

He wouldn't leave her mind and that was right. It had been her fault. If she hadn't befriended him, hadn't gotten the car or loaned it to him…

If.

She took a deep breath. She had to remain focused. She folded her arms as, despite the heat, a chill seemed to drift through her.

"Are you okay?"

Josh was right beside her. She wasn't sure how he had gotten there, and that thought was disconcerting.

"Yes." But the word was drawn out, not said with any confidence. And there was something odd in the way he looked at her. As if he understood…

"It'll be fine," he said without hesitation. "No matter what else is going on in your life, this is the chance of a lifetime."

Something had changed. There was an innuendo in his voice, as if he knew what she was afraid of. Of course, that was ridiculous. No one knew, no one except those who wanted her dead and a few others.

He steadied her with one hand on her arm. His grip was gentle, yet she suspected she wouldn't be able to break it. This wasn't the geek Josh she was comfortable with. This man was different. He made her heart race and her palms sweat.

"The heat," she murmured. What was wrong with her? It wasn't the heat and it wasn't claustrophobia. But she couldn't seem to quell her reluctance to move forward, to go anywhere near this cave. But it wasn't just the cave that was giving her jitters. It was her inability to control her racing heart every time he came near.

She could feel him behind her now, hear the sound of his feet on the wood, smell the faint scent of soap and something tangy, unlike earlier, it was something she couldn't identify it was so subtle. It toyed with her senses and sent odd tingles down her spine. She looked out over the railing where trees and vines seemed to twist, mesh and weave together into one writhing mass, where the animals—mammals, reptiles and birds alike—weaved through the tangled world of plants. The jungle was never ending, bracketed only by the distant limestone spears that punctured all that green and offered more treasures to the adventurous hiker. They also offered another way in.

Something tight twisted in her gut.

A bang sounded to her left, and she jumped and bit back a scream.

Behind her the woman screamed and then silence abruptly followed. Erin realized they hadn't exchanged names. It seemed wrong and haunting, and they were strange thoughts to flit through her mind in the few seconds it took before Josh had a grip on her arm and pushed her behind him.

"What...?" She wanted to break free, wanted to run.

"Quiet," he commanded in a voice that again didn't mesh with the man she had come to know. As he stayed her with one hand, she suspected he would restrain her if she moved at all.

He scanned the area, his hand on his side, the other continuing to hold her back. She looked down and saw the hint of dull black metal, a gun. His shirt shifted and then there was nothing.

Ridiculous. She had imagined the whole thing, not the bang, but the gun. There was no reason for him to be armed. He was an administrator and a reluctant tourist. It was ludicrous to think anything else. Still, her mind went back to that moment even as she stayed behind him and felt oddly safe.

It was a full minute before he released her, turning around at the same time. "Another damn lizard and a snapped-off branch." He pointed to the swaying grass and a tree branch that was lying half against the tree and half on the forest floor. Beyond that was the S-shaped trail of trampled foliage left behind by a reptile that was deceptively fast for its size.

"Monitor most likely."

She swallowed heavily as she thought of the lizard that could grow to six feet or more and was common in the area.

"Erin?"

"I'm all right, really," she snapped and immediately regretted the edge to her voice. "Maybe I… I just need some water."

"Here." He handed her an unopened bottle.

"No, that's yours." She reached into her pack. Nothing. She'd forgotten to pack water. That was inexcusable; she couldn't afford to forget any more than she could afford to be unobservant.

"I have two. Just in case," he said with a smile, breaking into her thoughts.

She looked at him with a combination of surprise and gratitude. "You must have been a Boy Scout as a kid." She'd obviously imagined the gun. She needed to take a step back. His earring caught her eye—ace of spades. She was seeing danger everywhere.

"Something like that," he said easily.

She looked into his eyes and for an odd moment she felt a little less alone. She wanted to get out of here, but instead she took a step closer to him, as if he could protect her.

Ridiculous, she told herself. There was no knight in shining armor. It was just her. She was alone.

Two days.

That was the amount of time he had to hold this position. Keep her here and keep her safe before a plane arrived to get them out.

The resort plane was unfeasible. Public transport, especially by plane, was just that, public and not the option he wanted. They needed to go back the way they had come, and transferring flights to do it was not wise. His thoughts backtracked to the previous night.

"What the hell happened to our ride out?" Josh asked, the cheap cell small and slippery in his hand.

"Too chancy. They've infiltrated Kuala Lumpur. One man for sure who could take your transport out at the knees," Vern replied.

"Good to know," Josh said drily.

"Bad news, pal. I know. Here's what you need to know. Sid Mylo is in Bangkok and with his lead out of the picture, it's slowed him down. And taking the man in Kuala Lumpur is only a matter of time."

"Meantime, there's intelligence in Bangkok. He'll get answers," Josh replied, his grip tight on the cell.

"Maybe. But we've been feeding him some bad leads, too. Hopefully he's picking those up."

"Hopefully. And if he isn't?"

"Then you do what you're paid to do. Get her the hell out of there," Vern replied.

"Reassuring," Josh muttered and disconnected. There wasn't much else to say. Bangkok was too close and their ride out feeling too far away. Right now there weren't any other options.

That had all been last night and a million miles away, or so he wished.

"Josh. You're not listening." There was a note of condemnation in her voice.

"Beautiful, aren't they?" he said, his attention again on her as the first stream of bats began their early evening exit for feeding. The sky soon darkened with more and more bats as they emerged from the enormous cave that he knew could easily hold a 747.

His eyes went skyward as one hand rested lightly on her shoulder.

She didn't push his hand away; instead, her attention remained on the sky and the bats coming out of the cave in one awe-inspiring, massive cloud. He looked in that direction but what he thought of was how her skin was warm, how the jut of her shoulder teased his palm, how her skin might feel like silk. He let his attention stray only slightly before he reeled it in, keeping an eye on the movements around him while appearing to marvel at the sight that everyone else was enthralled with.

She was watching—appearing to watch, anyway, but he knew that her mind wasn't really there. He could feel it in the tense way she held herself. He would have liked to know what she was thinking. He assumed she was still fearful, still considering her options, still thinking about when she needed to bolt. What he knew for sure was that she was tense. He wanted to knead the soft skin and ease the tension from her.

He put his free hand over his eyes as if to get a better view. It was an amazing sight, but one he'd seen on a previous mission during which he'd killed two rogue former KGB agents. His familiarity with Malaysia was one of the reasons he'd been called on.

The wrinkle-lipped bats were a black mass. Their squeaking seemed to fill the evening sky. In a way it was oddly surreal. The cloud of bats made him feel as if he were a tourist like the others. He reached for her hand, tentatively brushing his palm against her fingers. She didn't flinch or pull her hand away. His index finger brushed against her thumb. She tensed, and he held his breath, hoping she'd allow that one bit of contact.

They stood watching wave after wave of bats exit the cave. Their wings seemed to chafe the evening sky, their squeals echoing hollowly around them.

"Unbelievable," she said when the last of the animals trailed from the cave. The Japanese couple smiled at them and chatted happily as they followed behind on the long hike back.

Thirty minutes later they were at the resort. In a way it had all been oddly anticlimactic.

Josh looked at his watch.

Time was slipping away.

Chapter Fourteen

"I need a fly-in at exactly 19:00 hours, eight hours from now."

"You've made contact. Got her panting after you."

"Made contact," Josh said shortly. He didn't have time for Wade's chauvinistic and rather outdated humor, but Wade was from another generation and despite a youthful appearance, a few decades older than Josh's twenty-eight. That aside, Wade was his and Erin's ticket out of this place.

"You're okay?" Wade asked. "Haven't heard from you in months."

"Back-to-back assignments."

"Look, we'll talk after this. Get together. I've missed you, buddy."

"Sounds like a plan," Josh replied. He thought back to his conversation with Vern and what he'd learned and how it was not something to be shared with Wade. "I could use a few drinks, some laughs."

"Say no more."

Josh disconnected, thinking how much he missed just the friendship side of their relationship. Wade Gair had flown him in and out of hot spots since he'd first become a CIA operative. The two of them had trained together, military training first and then the more specialized training for the infiltration that their jobs demanded. Wade had been a latecomer to the CIA, arriving after a career in policing. In that time, and despite their age difference, they had become not just colleagues but friends.

His hand grazed the rail. It was muggy from the rain the previous night. The jungle was oddly quiet, which he found disturbing, almost ominous. A gecko skirted along the opposite railing and a multi-colored parrot-size bird stared at him from a nearby tree. He had no idea what kind of bird it was. He only knew that it was no threat and gorgeous. He scanned the area ahead. The pool was to his right, bracketed by lounge chairs and bordered by concrete. The rectangle of crystalline blue seemed to stretch endlessly. Empty, it was mesmerizingly still. A door shut on the main common area and a slight woman wearing the colorless dress of an employee came out carrying a tray. Again, no threat.

The click of a latch, and he turned but knew without a visual it was Erin.

She frowned when she saw him. There was something else in her look that had him pushing away from the railing, going to her.

"What's wrong?"

"I've looked everywhere. The common area, out here, everywhere…"

"Everywhere?" Had he lost his touch? How had she ended up out here without his knowledge? Without… There was no time for second-guessing. "What did you lose?"

"A picture." She hesitated as if she were going to say something else and then thought better of it.

"Picture?" His brows drew together. Considering everything that had happened to her, he couldn't comprehend the importance of one picture.

"My father. He died when I was young. I know it may sound silly, but I carry his picture with me." She hesitated. "I always have. And now it's gone." There was a haunted look in her eyes and a pallor to her face that made him realize that this was real, a fear unlike the case of claustrophobia-that-wasn't yesterday. Whatever it was that was attached to that picture was as real as her flight to Mulu. And, he realized, despite the gravity of her situation, in this moment possibly more important.

He thought of the beaded earring in his pocket. He'd carried it for five years now, almost since he'd first joined the CIA. A talisman that he'd admitted to no one and a reminder of his mother who'd died five years ago, the victim of a home invasion and brutal rape.

"Did you have it after the Deer Cave yesterday?"

"I'm not sure."

He glanced at his watch, although in a pinch he could approximate time by the position of the sun. There was no tour going to Deer Cave this morning and no tourists going on their own. He'd spoken to Tenuk and gotten a full account of the day's activities. A group of tourists was going with a guide to one of the farther caves. They'd left more than an hour ago. Since the resort wasn't at peak capacity, there were only a few left behind.

"I'm going to Deer Cave," she said with determination and as if she had read his mind. "I can't lose that picture."

"Erin, I don't think you—"

"That I should go there? Alone," she finished as if they were an old married couple. "It's okay, Josh. Broad daylight."

He pushed away from the railing. He didn't like the

idea of her heading anywhere alone, especially to one of the caves. It wouldn't happen.

"I have to go, Josh." And there was steel in her voice. "That picture is everything to me. There are no others."

"What do you mean? It's not digital? Scanned?"

She shook her head.

No others. Josh was flabbergasted. In this day of computers, that there wasn't a scanned picture on a disk drive somewhere was unfathomable.

"I have a copy on my computer, but this one..." She bit her lip again. "He gave it to me. He..."

He got it. Her father had touched it with his hands. And while that might seem overly sentimental to others, he could see the importance. He knew from his research that her father had died of a brain aneurysm when Erin was twelve.

He could see it was important enough for her to forget the danger that was so close, important enough for her to focus on the search rather than her plan to leave. The exit strategy was clear. He'd seen the map in her bag. Smart, using a physical map rather than relying on traceable technology. But her plan wouldn't happen. She'd be out of here before she took action into her own hands. By the end of today she'd know who he was and welcome his protection. It was a comforting thought, but one way or another she was leaving tonight. In the meantime, they were still in the clear. Tenuk had reported less than thirty minutes ago that his sources along the river had seen nothing. So he'd humor her on a mission that he could see was of high sentimental importance.

Within the past thirty minutes, the first plane of the day had landed as scheduled and before it landed a quick background check on all of them had brought up nothing but innocuous tourists—two Americans, both women and neither travelling together, a French single woman and a Malaysian couple with two kids. And the pilot had been doing this run for a long time, his skin swarthy from years of sun, his eyes hidden within the folds of skin that had wrinkled in late middle age. None of them was a threat, yet going back on this path was ill-advised despite the signs pointing otherwise. It wasn't facts he'd garnered but rather a gut reaction. He'd learned to trust gut reactions every bit as much, but how did he explain that to Erin. Truth at this point could damage the trust he'd already built between them.

"I often think if Dad hadn't died, my sister, Sarah…" She hesitated. "I'm sorry. You don't know her and now I'm burdening you with stupid family history."

"It's not stupid if it means something to you," he assured her. He knew she had booked a boat ticket tomorrow. There was no way she was leaving here by boat or any other means by herself. He had hours to reveal the truth and get her to buy in. He pushed the thoughts aside and smiled encouragingly. "Tell me."

"Sarah had a tough time growing up. She didn't fit. She was shy, introspective, different—and kids bullied her." She shook her head. "Look, I'm sorry. You don't know what I'm talking about and it's not relevant."

He merely nodded. He knew exactly who Sarah was. Four years younger than Erin and the reason she was on the run. There was nothing he didn't know about her, including that her sister was now in protective custody.

"If you want to talk about it," he ventured.

"No." She waved her hand. "I'm sorry. It's just… I have to find that picture."

Thirty minutes later they were back on the path heading to Deer Cave.

They didn't go far or fast. She moved slowly, her attention shifting from right to left and into the dense foliage that bracketed the path. He had never seen her so jumpy, not even on that first day after all the horror of the explosion. Even then, despite the haunted look in her eyes, she had projected a composure that he had admired. Now he could see the tension in the way her shoulders were set and in her silence. And it was not over men with guns and a death wish, but rather one simple photograph. In a way it was as oddly endearing as it was disconcerting.

"I can't lose it," she muttered, twisting her hands together.

His gaze swept the jungle, the walkway and her.

"Tell me about your father," he said as a way to disperse some of the tension. She was working herself into a state that threatened to be exhausting.

"I wasn't close to him," she said through tight lips.

That surprised him considering her reaction to the missing picture.

"I know." She laughed, a dry, humorless sound that sent a sliver of warning straight to his gut. "You're wondering, why am I in such a knot about this picture?" She stopped, stuffed her hands into the pockets of her shorts and looked somewhere past him, as if the answer were in the ever-changing yet never-changing jungle.

"He was your father. Understandable."

"I think it was because I missed so much. I never really knew him. He was on the road a good portion of my childhood." She pulled her hands from her pockets. "This is all irrelevant. We're wasting time. The tours begin in an hour. It won't be so easy to look at our leisure then."

"But if you don't find the picture you still have the memory."

She stopped and swung around. "Thanks, Josh." She hesitated. "For everything."

"I haven't done much—"

"You've done more than you know," she interrupted with a hand on his arm. Her touch was hot and connected in a way that he wanted to reciprocate, to touch her back, to press her against the railing, to…

He put his hands on her upper arms, pulling her closer.

She didn't stop him. Instead, there was an oddly puzzled look, a softer cast to her gaze.

His right hand cupped her cheek and his lips met hers. His tongue caressed the velvet skin, parting it as his hand moved downward, slipping along her ribs, flirting with the edge of her breast, imagining what it would be like to taste her there.

She moaned, and he pulled her closer, his crotch hard and tight against her belly, his arm around her waist, his tongue plundering her mouth.

Security.

Damn it, he thought.

"I'm sorry." He pushed her gently away, steadying her but putting distance between them with his arms.

She pulled away from him, stumbled back, her eyes confused and clouded.

"Sorry?" she asked, and her hand swept the curve of her waist and then dropped. "I… You're right. That shouldn't have happened."

"I hope this doesn't stand in the way of our friendship."

"No." She stumbled. "No. Of course not. I shouldn't have, either. I…I need to find that picture."

He took her hand. "C'mon, let's keep going."

It was minutes of silence, of him trailing her, watching her and watching the jungle around them before he spoke.

"Where are you going after here?" It was an inane question, but it was safe.

"I'm not sure," she said. Her eyes scanned the walk as

if the picture would miraculously appear in the middle of a path that had seen too many footprints since yesterday.

And from the tone of her voice he knew that she was sure.

It was almost time to reveal the truth. That her destination was not what she thought, and he was not who she believed.

Almost.

A ray of sun shone down and seemed not only blindingly bright but reminded him of their narrow time frame, how the morning was already aging out, and the situation that could heat up at any minute. He looked left, then right, his hand ready to grab his weapon at any time.

They were at the mouth of Deer Cave. The jungle was oddly quiet and the bats safe in their rooftop hollows, sleeping until the rush for feeding tonight. It seemed despite millions of breathing, sleeping bats, they were alone.

"I hate to say it, but that picture is more than likely lost."

"It can't be, Josh." She shook her head.

"You didn't go into this cave, so there's no point going in now." And despite his words and the hint that she had a choice, there was none. She wouldn't be entering that cave with or without him.

"You're right." She hugged her arms to her chest and looked so forlorn he almost took her into his arms without thought.

A crack broke the tension of his thoughts. The sound was foreign and unlike the sounds that he had heard in the time they had been at the resort. He tensed, prepared to act, to protect her.

One hand was on his gun, the other on her elbow.

There was a split second of silence and then a branch snapped hollowly as something shrieked in the heart of the forest. The crack was followed by a flash of light and an echo that volleyed in the brush, reverberating through the dense foliage that closed around them. A warning, a missed shot. He suspected the latter and dove into action.

"Get down!"

He had her around the waist, hitting the ground first and rolling with her. He lifted his head from where they lay flat to the wooden walkway. There was silence. Worse, he couldn't see through the thick canopy of long-leafed plants and tall grass that bordered the walkway and seemed to close in around them. They blocked any view he might have. He didn't know what view the shooter had.

Josh had his Glock in one hand. He silently indicated that she should remain where she was. Her eyes confirmed that she understood. She lay motionless, but he could feel her tension and knew she was poised to run.

He scanned the area, searching. The whisper of the jungle began to heat up and something shrilled again, as if warning of change, of danger deep in its depths.

He drew in a tense breath as he considered what that single shot had meant. Was it a warning or a way of drawing them out and off the path? It was all the data he had, and he had to make a decision. To remain on the wooden boardwalk was to remain in the open—a target. They had to get back to the resort, to safety.

His analysis was broken by another shot to the left, but seemingly distant enough that Josh suspected the shooter was firing at random. The odds were high that he didn't have a clear view of them, any more than they did of him. But the second shot was too close and within seconds of that shot, Josh had his arm around her and was again rolling along the wooden pathway to the right and toward a dip that took them closer to the jungle floor. With the shots coming from behind them, there was no way they could go back the way they came. They had to move ahead, and the nearby cave was no option.

He thought of the river in Clearwater Cave, a back entrance that could lead them to the resort and potentially to safety. Safety, that was, if he could keep the target unharmed and stop their pursuer.

He ran through the layout of the cave, the path and the suspected location of the shooter. They were far enough ahead, and the pathway angled for a few hundred feet in a way that would be to their advantage. And with the pursuer behind them, they were being pushed forward and that made forward the logical way to go. He couldn't judge the distance, but whoever it was, was well concealed by jungle.

He rose with a tight grip on her hand.

"Let's move."

He met resistance but he'd expected that and was ready to power through. He turned and with gritted teeth said, "Look, Erin, I know who you are."

"Who are you?" she whispered, her voice tight, almost strangled.

"CIA."

"No." The word was small and soft in the vastness of the jungle.

She seemed paralyzed with disbelief, fright—he wasn't sure which. He needed to pull her out of it. Shock her.

"They want you dead." He took her arm. "I'm here to make sure that doesn't happen."

She seemed unable to comprehend what he was saying. He went for a figurative slap.

"Emma is dead." He didn't have to qualify with a surname. Her look told him everything he needed to know. She knew who Emma was.

Her face went pale, paler than it had been only seconds before.

The words were shocking, but he knew she needed something to galvanize her into action. It was a brutal way for her to find out about the woman who had been an acquaintance—a friend, he suspected. But he didn't have time to use pretty words or soothe her shattered calm. He had to get her up and get them moving. They'd been discovered and they needed to get the hell out fast.

She pulled her hand free.

"Look," he gritted. "There's no time to offer proof. You have two choices. Trust me or…" He nodded his head backward where it was obvious only death waited.

She stood there almost rocking on her heels. He could see the indecision, the unwillingness to trust any further, and he didn't blame her.

It had been seconds really that she wavered, although it seemed longer. Suddenly, her indecision was gone. Now he no longer had to tug at her—she was moving alongside him, pushing ahead, running. They were moving along the boardwalk path that had once seemed so civilized, so harmless, so…

He could hear her breaths, heavy with an edge that bordered on labored. He had her running full-out.

One minute and then two; he knew it wasn't physical exhaustion that would take her down quickly but the emotional panic that overlaid it all. She wasn't trained to deal with a flight-or-fight moment, no matter how much she'd upped her exercise routine.

Four minutes in they rounded a familiar bend where the walkway's elevation lowered. His gaze cast down into the jungle, waiting for the break when the jungle met the path.

He stopped suddenly. They couldn't run forever. They

needed shelter, and that shelter was looming ahead of them in the sweating foliage of the rain forest.

"Are you okay?" he asked.

She nodded, panting, and in her glazed, fear-stricken eyes he saw, or maybe hoped he saw something that hadn't been there before—trust edged with a little desperation.

He went to ground, dropping to the wooden walkway, pulling her down beside him, their feet dangling over the rich vine-and-brush-layered jungle. Here it was a little less dense. And only a few feet away they could get lost. He would have to carefully follow the walkway above them.

They were on the other side from where the shot had come. They could hide as easily as their pursuer. He doubted if whoever was after them had any more jungle knowledge than he did. If it was Sid, he suspected from his notes on the man, less. But that aside the man was good and would make up for it in other areas.

"Jump!"

She nodded, and with that he pushed off, her hand firmly in his, her body aligned perfectly with his. They landed with a thump. He released her hand as he rolled and was immediately on his feet. He held out his hand; there was no hesitation as she gave him hers. He helped her to her feet and began to jog ahead to where the trees grew thicker, the foliage deeper, where they might be more hidden. Still, the noise of their movements couldn't be covered. Instead of the thud of hikers on wood, there was the rustle of brush being moved aside and a different sound to their footsteps. He looked up and could see the path directly to his right. The sun was screened by the walkway and shadows were thick in the foliage. But still it felt too open.

"This way," he hissed. "To Clearwater Cave," he said in answer to her unspoken question.

She didn't say anything, and he admired the fact that she instinctively knew to be silent, to keep up.

The cave was where he had the best chance of defending them and where they had the best chance of escape. But that cave was twenty minutes away on a walk. That time would be shortened by a run but through jungle and with her smaller steps and endurance, it was still a good distance away. Overhead there were only jungle sounds— a bird calling for a mate, the thud of a branch dropping to the forest floor—but behind them there was nothing.

It was over ten minutes before they stood below the cave and another minute before they had climbed the steps and were at the entrance of the cave. Behind them there had been silence more disturbing than the earlier gunshot.

He held her back with one arm around her waist.

A minute, two passed.

He nodded to her and they stepped into the damp coolness, the rustle of bats overhead and the feeling that they had entered another world.

He silently counted their steps as soon as they passed the entrance and the light began to fade. A generator sat at the entrance to provide light for the tours. It wasn't running. Instead, there was an uneasy stillness filled with the rustling of the creatures of the dark and the bats. Their presence was everywhere as the darkness closed in, as he and Erin moved away from the entrance and the light faded. He continued to count their steps.

Twenty.

Thirty-five.

Her palm was warm and trusting against his. Briefly, he wondered how much of that was illusion, his want of her trust, and how much was real. It didn't matter. He shifted his hand, taking a stronger grip on hers. The fetid scent of the other occupants of this cave was oddly comforting, as if the bats stood between them and danger.

Forty-five.

They were smaller steps than he had taken before. He'd factored that in the previous night—her steps weren't as large as his and he was already pushing her to her limits and about to ask for more.

Fifty.

Not far enough to be safe from gunfire but far enough to be out of sight in the shadowy darkness. He hugged them as close to the inside railing as they could get, she on the inside, near the rock, and he on the outside, where danger could lurk. He'd considered going directly to their area of least defense because it was also the one that cloaked them the best as no light reached there. But it meant going across the uncharted floor where the stalagmites made walking treacherous. That wasn't for her.

A shadow moved in the entrance that was now well behind them. Still, it was a light-filled beacon although the light no longer reached them.

Josh's hand went to the Glock. "Get down," he hissed. "And keep moving."

A shot rang out.

The small flashlight he carried had subtly marked their path not just for them but the killer who was following them. Another shot this time to his left.

He clicked off the beam.

A sliver of light cut through the darkness. It wasn't sunlight and it came from the entrance.

"Run!"

Chapter Fifteen

He could feel her eyes on him and sensed the fear vibrating from her. There was no time for comfort, for consoling. "Go." He tried to couch as much confidence as he could in his voice. If he could he would have taken her fear and eliminated it like he eventually would their pursuer.

"Stay on the walkway to the river," he said in a harsh whisper as he gave her a slight push and then moved forward, placing himself between her and whoever was after them. He could see a shadow at the entrance, the outline of a man. He lifted his Glock and shot—a warning more than anything.

The answering shots rang out—one, two, three. Josh counted them off so he could time as closely as possible the moment when a reload would be needed. And while he counted he turned and ran, following Erin, heading for the river and their escape.

Ten shots.

If he'd guessed right, there were five to seven bullets left depending on what kind of magazine the bastard had. His mind reeled with possibilities. He stopped, assessing the situation.

Nothing. Only silence.

He moved forward quietly now, waiting, listening. Then he deliberately kicked a rock that pitched forward landing hollowly somewhere ahead of him. Another shot. There were four to six left. He couldn't be sure. He scuffled his feet, not too much to create suspicion that this might be a diversion, but enough to focus the killer's attention on him rather than on Erin.

The silence was too long.

The bastard was reloading.

Erin was far enough ahead, out of range. He could hear her moving forward as he'd instructed, but he could no longer see her.

He leaned down, felt around for another rock, picked up one and then two. He threw one. The stone rattled in a hollow clatter just ahead of him and to his left as it bounced along the cave floor. He hit the ground as another shot fired in the direction of the rock he'd just thrown.

There was a deathly stillness that seemed strangely alive, as if the cave breathed around him.

He threw the second rock and began to move forward toward the river. There was an odd whirring like a faint clapping, seeming more distant than it was, as the bats were disturbed and a few began to fly around.

He bent down, jumping lightly off the walkway and to the floor of the cave. He moved carefully, quietly, picking his way along the treacherous floor, heading to the river and Erin.

He counted his steps, choreographing them to the night before. He was within fifty feet of the river. Already he could sense it by the increase in moisture in the air and that odd smell that wasn't quite as dank as the rest of the cave. He stopped, looked behind as something moved to his left.

A light flickered briefly but long enough for him to pinpoint their tracker. He fired. There was a thud, then the sound of something falling. He'd made contact. At least, he hoped he had.

Seconds ticked by and there was nothing, only a hollow emptiness, silence so deep that it had him silencing his own movements, listening and looking ahead for Erin.

Was whoever pursued them gravely injured?

Dead?

He moved forward as the cave floor smoothed out and the ceiling lowered. He couldn't see her. "Be there," he muttered and hoped that she hadn't veered off the path, that he hadn't missed her.

Where was she?

"Josh," she whispered very close to him.

He reached up toward the walkway, where he could see the dim glimmer of flesh. His fingers brushed against her hand. He could see the whites of her eyes in the dark, in the muted flare of his flashlight as he shone it through his sleeve. And what he saw looked stark and very afraid.

He gave her hand a gentle tug, felt her nod in understanding as she scooted to the edge of the walkway, dangled her legs over as he reached up and lifted her down. Behind them the silence was somehow more ominous than anything that had come before. He took her hand and they began to pick their way forward. The sound of water dripping overhead and the dank cool feel of the rock intensified as they came closer to the river. He squeezed her hand, trying to transfer courage to her or at the least trust in him. For what he was about to ask her to do, swim in the dark, and finally going underwater. Doing that might take all the courage she had.

Behind them, there were no shots and Josh wished there had been. Then at least he could have tracked the bastard, known if he was getting closer or had gotten lucky and killed him.

"Can you swim?" he asked.

"No. I took lessons, but…"

"No?" He stopped, and she bumped into him. Lessons. She should be able to swim. Irrelevant. She couldn't. He redirected his mind from the problem to the solution.

She clutched his hand so tightly that he thought he would lose feeling. "I can float, but…" Her voice shook.

Gently, he unpeeled her fingers from his. "I'll do the swimming for both of us."

Her breath was soft, hitching in the bleak darkness. Behind them a killer might still lurk and there was no time to bolster her courage. They had to get out of here, fear or not.

He took a breath, his mind checking off the options, the alternatives. There was none. There was only one thing to do.

He squeezed her hand as they turned around a large boulder, the final marker that told him they were there. His hand felt along now in the darkness. He flicked on his flashlight as they were now shielded from the entrance and from the killer by distance and the twists and turns they had taken to get here.

If his calculation was right, they would soon be within a few feet from where the cave floor opened up and the underground river began.

Around them the damp, dank walls seemed to almost breathe a collective sigh. Beside him, he could hear Erin's soft, almost hitching breathing. His hand went to her arm and in the process brushed the soft rise of her breast. He felt the rapid beat of her heart, and the warm, sweet scent that was distinctly her seemed to surround him. He couldn't help it—in this microsecond lull of safety, he pulled her tight against him, pressed his lips against hers. The kiss was hard and deep as his tongue explored her mouth, and she clung to him, her heart pounding against his. Behind him he could hear the steady drip of water, see nothing but darkness and smell the musty scent of water too long in an enclosed space.

He broke the kiss, his hands on her shoulder. "Hang on to me and don't let go no matter what happens."

He bent down and felt her hands on his shoulders and her legs close around his waist. "It's underwater. Take a deep breath when I tell you."

One minute was what he had timed for this first leg. An eternity for anyone who hadn't practiced holding their breath for any length of time, especially in a situation where fear made the body crave more oxygen. He ran a hand along her forearm. "Ready?"

"Ready."

He felt her draw in her breath and her slight weight press against his back. He took a breath. Turned and nodded to her before he jumped in with her clinging to his back.

The initial push into the water was more difficult than he'd thought. Suddenly her weight seemed heavier, more than he anticipated, and his shin scraped against rock. Pain sliced through him, stabbing up his leg, and he hoped it was nothing serious.

Water closed over his head as they went under.

The water was surprisingly warm as they sank. Warmer than he remembered it being the previous night. He began making powerful strokes, pushing them upward and forward. His lungs began to burn as they pushed toward the point where he knew that they would begin to ache for lack of oxygen. He hoped she could hang on until they broke the surface.

He counted seconds as he had done when he had run the first trial of this water escape. He allowed for an extra few seconds, knowing he was swimming slower with Erin on his back.

Twenty-one.

Twenty-two.

Twenty-three.

Water pressed heavily on him and now her weight seemed so light as not to be there. The only reassurance that she was still there was her arm that was around his neck and pressing so hard that it hurt. He reached up and brushed her forearm with his hand, a silent warning to change her grip. She shifted her arm, taking the pressure off his throat.

Twenty-four.

Twenty-five.

They were just beneath the surface now. He was within half a minute of reaching his endurance and that meant she was at the end of hers.

Thirty.

Thirty-one.

He'd mentally counted out forty when he forced them above the surface to where they were out of the main interior of the cave, into the quiet subsidiary that led through tight rock, another turn that was completely under the rock and then out into another cave area and finally close to the entrance of the resort and hopefully safety.

She gasped, her grip on him tight as he surfaced. He wanted to ask if she was okay, but he could only tentatively squeeze one hand and suck in a silent breath as he took long, sure strokes, floating and pushing forward in turns, as the water seemed to close in around them, insulating them from the danger that lurked behind. Ahead he could see light and hoped nothing was there to meet them or they would be screwed. His mind ran through the options.

His muscles screamed now with the extra weight. Swimming had never been his forte. She shifted, and he gritted his teeth, expecting her to lose her grip and slide off. He prepared for rescue. Instead, her grip tightened.

She was every bit as tenacious as he, he thought with an inward smile. They'd make it out. All he had to do was keep swimming. Behind them there was a disturbing silence filled only by the lap of water.

There was no going backward, no turning to face anyone. There was only escape in that slash of light ahead of him. From there he needed a plan and he kept swimming, his mind on a plan of action that would get her the hell out of here.

"Take a breath. We're going under one more time."

Her answer was a tightening of her grip on his shoulders.

"On three."

Water closed around them as tight and as urgent as his thoughts. He had to move fast, get to the resort and get her out. But two things stood in the way of that: the gunman behind him and the woman on his back. Of the two things, it was the woman he was most concerned about. A life-and-death matter was one thing, but when they emerged from this cave how would he convince her that he was the only way to safety?

Chapter Sixteen

Erin clung to his back, one hand now fisting his shirt, her other arm around his neck. Was she holding too tight? Would she choke him? Should she let go, and if she did would she drown? They were crazy thoughts, uncontrolled, and she couldn't stop them. The thoughts, the fear, all of it ran rampant through her.

Her eyes were pinched shut.

She was underwater, unable to breathe, unable to move, her only chance of survival, Josh.

Hair twisted across her face, covering her nose like a sheet of plastic wrap. Her cheeks puffed out like those of a blowfish. She was too terrified to release her grip on his shirt, or maybe it was his shoulder that her nails were now digging into, she didn't know. All she knew was that she wasn't letting go, ever.

She wanted to drag in air. Her lungs burned and fear made her want to breathe in the worst way.

Her hand gripped his shirt so hard that her fingers ached.

In the swirl of water that threatened to drown her the past flooded her mind as if it were more comfortable than the present and the reality that they could both die.

She could hear the taunts of the children.

That had been so long ago. She'd been eleven.

She could see her sister's frightened face.

She could feel her own fear that day.

"No," she'd screamed as she'd watched almost in slow motion. Water had nearly killed her sister. Those children had pushed her off the bridge. Pushed her sister into the river. She was back again, in that river, struggling to save her sister. Then, the only thing she'd had was luck on her side and a river with wide, shallow shoals along its banks.

She opened her eyes and reality flooded in. She squeezed them shut. Her lungs begged for air and she wrestled the fear that demanded she take a breath, underwater or not.

She shifted and found herself sliding. There was a moment of panic as the water seemed to pull at her, trying to tear her away before his hand reached back and steadied her.

She locked her ankles around his middle. Well-toned, hard, the impressions flitted through her mind as easily as the water ran over her skin, caressing it in an odd way, disturbingly cool and detached. Water ran slickly between his skin and hers, making her hold on him tenuous. She concentrated on hanging on, surviving this moment, getting out of the water and not getting shot. As for the rest... She needed a plan and, damn it, it appeared she might have run out of options. Her plan was him and clinging to him. This wasn't a plan. This was desperation.

They broke the surface and she struggled to draw air, gasping and fighting for control. Her lungs ached and she coughed, but her hold on him was almost unbreakable. He was swimming with slow, strong strokes, taking them away from the threat behind them.

"Hang on," he said in a hoarse whisper, as if that command were necessary, as if she would let go before he got them the hell out of this river.

To her right, not three feet away, was a ledge that seemed to slice through the water. It was narrow, she suspected too narrow for two. The entrance was close. She could see light maybe twenty feet ahead. Water still stood between them and the exit, and for a moment they seemed to bob in a swirl of current that came out of nowhere. Water lapped over her face, and she choked, fought to bite back a cough that might alert whoever was pursuing them of their presence.

Her pursuer.

A tremor ran through her at the unnecessary reminder.

"Grab the ledge. Can you get it?" he asked, breaking into her thoughts.

Her hand reached out. Her fingers shook. She took a breath. There was no time for hesitation. She felt slick rock. She wouldn't be able to hold on. She...

"Use me as a float."

Not following his instruction wasn't a choice; surviving was. She couldn't think. She reached out. Her heart hammered.

She couldn't do this.

She was starting to slide and there was only one place to go—under.

Then her hands were on the ledge, she was half-off his back. It felt as if a quarter of her body lay on the ledge, and her fingernails clawed rock, while the weight of her body threatened to drag her back down into the darkness, into the river alone—without Josh.

Where was he?

"Josh." She wanted to yell. Instead, it was only a terrified whisper as she was shoved from beneath, pushed, hands on her butt pushing her up and...

She managed to get a grip on the edge of rock and pulled herself the remainder of the way out of the water finally, scrambling, trying to push her legs over the ledge, and within seconds she was there. The slick rock was cool beneath her wet clothes. Her heart hammered, and she searched the water. There was no one, he was…

Gone!

"Damn, Josh…" She wanted to scream his name, as the terror of what and who pursued her beat down on her, hard, relentless and deadly in the darkness.

She was terrified for herself, for him. She couldn't go back into that water, not alone.

Had he drowned?

Left her?

She almost choked on her fear.

Then he broke the surface. She could see him faintly, the outline, the idea of him. Her heart hammered in a way it never had before. She had been afraid like she'd never been before.

She took a deep breath as he reached up and pulled himself out of the water, landing with an odd thump on the ledge beside her.

She thought he'd disappeared, left—worse, drowned—and she was alone. It frightened her like nothing in the months of flight from the Anarchists had. She'd feared for his safety, for his life. And for the first time she'd feared that she couldn't do this alone.

A shiver raced through her.

"Erin." His finger trailed softly, reassuringly along her cheek. He flicked on the flashlight, illuminating her face and lifting the shadows from his eyes.

She clutched her arms beneath her breasts and looked away from him. She scanned the area for where they would go next. Another shiver shook her. Ahead was the pool where many tourists often ended their tour of the caves. At least that's what he had said. Everything she knew about how to get out of here was what Josh had said.

She'd never felt so helpless, so dependent. She took in a quick gulping breath and squeezed her hands into fists. She unlocked her hands, biting back another shiver.

He stood up, water dripping from his hair and from his clothing, and his presence seemed to fill the narrow ledge. He held out his hand.

She didn't take it, not immediately. The truth was she couldn't stand. Her legs were shaking too much. She willed the shaking to stop. But just thinking it, just taking a deep breath didn't steady her nerves, not that quickly and they didn't have time. She knew that.

"We've got to keep going," he said in that short, decisive way that was nothing like the Josh of their initial meetings. "Details later."

She nodded.

This was a man not used to being ignored. This was a man used to being in charge.

Josh was no tourist. He'd made that quite clear. But the question that threatened her very safety was what did he want? The only thing that was clear was that in the moment he wanted her alive.

Alive was what she'd fought for all these months. She took the hand Josh offered and for the moment, for as long as it was necessary, she gave him her trust.

Chapter Seventeen

The cave was directly behind them and a pool of water in front. The sun was blinding after the darkness of the cave and the blackness of the underground river. Now they stood poised on a rock ledge fifteen feet up and faced more water.

"Jump," he ordered.

Despite the command, he knew she couldn't, not immediately. She was faced with two terrifying options—potential death behind them and the fear of water, and its association with death, in front of her. He could feel the fear and doubt and see that she was frozen. It was a normal reaction, instinctive—the will to survive. But she had no choice. The grip on her hand told her so. He tried to communicate everything he couldn't say into that palm-to-palm connection. He squeezed her hand once, looked at her and said, "You can do this. One, two…"

"Three."

The counting was what kept him focused, grounded and he hoped it did the same for her. It was a fleeting thought as they were in the air on three, leaping from the ledge that skirted a small opening from the cave into a pool of water, crystal clear and cool. Again, water closed over their heads. He could feel her fingernails biting into the back of his hand. He squeezed her hand, his other arm pushing them back up.

They broke the surface. His hand still had an iron grip on hers as he turned to face her, one arm holding her up, the other treading water. Her face was red as she fought not to gasp for air, trying to remain silent, aware that there was still a threat somewhere behind them.

He wiped a drop of water from his brow and then traced a finger gently down her cheek.

"That man…" she began and she shivered despite the warm evening air.

He knew she was biting back panic, and still he slammed her with the truth.

"Dead," he said bluntly. Although for the flight through the river he'd maintained a belief that they were still being followed, known the possibility existed and pushed himself because of it, now there was no reason to believe so. There would have been more shots if the man weren't dead. Instead, there had been silence for too many minutes. And prior there'd been an odd thud, the sound of a body falling, hard to confuse with anything else.

She nodded, her teeth worrying her bottom lip. The water lapped at their waists as they waded out. As she stepped out of the water, he let go of her hand.

"We'll circumvent the resort, go in off the trail. Go to my room. It's the safest right now," he said.

"Is it true?" She hesitated, her face almost pained. "What you said? That you're CIA?"

He knew that his silence was all the answer she needed.

Her face seemed to lose color. If she had been pale before, her face was a death mask now. It was as if every bit of emotion, of life, had been sucked out of her.

"I'm here to take you home," he added in case that hadn't been clear.

She shook her head violently and took a stumbling step back.

He reached out to her, and she knocked his hand away, her wet hair swinging across her cheek and making an odd slapping sound.

"The Anarchists won't touch you. You're safe. You'll be in protective custody."

"No!"

"I'm afraid you don't understand, Erin. You don't have a choice."

"I'm under arrest?"

"No, of course not. But you're not free to go, either. I'll accompany you the whole way." He held her gaze. "Let me get you out of Mulu." He stepped back from the reality of the rest of where he was taking her. "I know you have plans, but the river is not safe."

Surprise was in her eyes and in the lift of her brow.

"The man who was tracking you wasn't their best." He shook his head. "And there's someone else, another assassin en route."

"More than one... Oh, my God." She squatted down, defeated.

He suspected her legs were unable to hold her and he felt for her. She was one small woman, untrained in this kind of thing, with men after her who were able to track and take out the most skilled individuals.

"I can't do this. There's no place where they won't find me."

"There's one place," he replied.

"Where?"

He held out his hand. "With me."

She looked up at him and gave him a single nod of her head and, he suspected, all the trust she had in that moment.

She gave him her hand.

If her trust wouldn't last beyond getting her out of Mulu, he'd face that later. In the meantime, he wasn't sure how much he trusted her new resolve. He definitely wasn't releasing her hand. He'd learned a long time ago not to trust any of his assignments. And that was all she was, an assignment. And if he told himself that often enough, he hoped it might be true.

"Josh!"

Her cry had him immediately on guard as he instinctively looked up.

Maybe forty feet away and twenty feet up, metal glinted in the light that dodged through the trees and it was clear that an armed man stood on the ledge. He stood slightly to the side, protected by the nondescript rock that hung into the jungle's vast reach. Josh registered size, hair color and matched him to a previous glimpse he'd gotten of their pursuer as his hand reached for his gun and his other pushed Erin behind him.

One shot and then two, the man dropped, his gun clattered partway down the rocks.

"Dead?" a small voice asked behind him.

"Dead," he confirmed as he spun her around. "Let's get out of here."

But only a few minutes into the hike that would take them back to the resort, she stopped, and he suspected she might be at her limit. They were alone except for the virulent life that hid in the jungle surrounding them.

"He's dead," she whispered. "Were there two?"

"No." He'd made a mistake. He'd thought he'd killed him once; he'd been wrong. His right hand clenched into a fist.

Unacceptable.

"Same man. He wasn't dead. He is now."

Tentatively, he touched her arm, the bare skin like velvet beneath his fingers. He'd dragged her through hell and she had said little. He tilted her chin with a forefinger, concerned that maybe she was in shock.

"Erin?"

Her lips quivered and a tear slipped down her cheek. He hadn't expected that; he suspected neither of them had.

"I'm out of my league," she murmured as her weight pressed against him as if her body had no will of its own. She looked up, and he looked down and somewhere in the middle their lips met. And once it had begun, he couldn't stop it. It was as if the shock and trauma that had just occurred needed the reaffirmation of life—they were alive. They had survived. The thoughts were only blips on his radar for her lips were full and moist against his. One hand skimmed the warm satin of her breast. Her nipple pebbled against his hand, and he realized she was braless.

He didn't say anything. He didn't need to. What he needed to do was get his hand off her breast, to lead them forward. There was no place for sexual antics with a dead man behind them. There was no place anywhere.

But he wanted the feel of her skin against his. Wanted it worse than he could remember ever wanting anything in his life. The danger, here in a place where this shouldn't happen and most of all with her—a woman whose curves he'd only imagined and had tentatively only explored the edges. His groin tightened at the thought of holding her, exploring her.

The timing was wrong.

He'd had his share of one-night stands and short-term relationships. He'd given his heart to no woman. And he definitely hadn't given his heart to Erin, but he suspected rather belatedly that while he might not have offered it, she might very well be in the process of a covert operation and be stealing it out from under him.

No.

She was a woman, not a covert operation. He pushed away and with the danger behind them gone, he began to move forward, not looking backward at her face, not willing to see what her eyes might reveal.

She was an assignment, no more, and while he wasn't willing to give his heart, he was more than willing to share his body.

Chapter Eighteen

One down. How many more to go?

He had pushed her to her limit and beyond, but they had finally made it back to the resort and relative safety. Josh's mind raced even as his senses were attuned to everything around him.

They entered the resort from the back. It was quiet as many of the tours were still an hour or two from completion. He looked at Erin. She was pale despite her time in Asia. Her hair hung free of its earlier ponytail. One piece of dark hair had dried into a curl and the rest hung straight. It was an odd thing to notice yet it was a relief to touch the edge of normal if only for a second.

"You're all right?" he asked softly.

She nodded as if speaking might be too much effort. She'd been quiet the whole walk back, as had he. He'd been planning and considering his next move; he suspected she might have been doing the same. He wanted to tell her there was no need. Instead, he had maintained the silence.

Tenuk met them, his hands fisted by his sides. "Son of a bitch! I didn't think you'd make it out. I was about to go in after you."

"We did. What the hell happened? We were compromised. We had the all clear." He looked Tenuk directly in the eye. "You gave it to us."

"I know." Tenuk shook his head. "Like you said, I gave that to you this morning. Damn it!" His fist clenched. "Faulty intelligence. No excuse. I'm just thankful you made it out alive."

Josh watched Tenuk closely while he listened for any changes around him.

"Came in on foot and by river. Took out two of my men before I was alerted that he'd slipped through the net." Tenuk ran a thick hand through his hair. "I didn't find out soon enough to warn you. I take it you managed. No injuries, I mean."

"I managed," Josh said.

"Can't keep all angles covered. I know that now. The river and the jungle, it's too easy to come in under the wire."

"Makes sense. Just wish you'd been aware of that sooner. Would have saved me a lot of grief." What he had to remember were the men the Anarchists had now hired were more than likely every bit as experienced in tracking and slipping under the wire as he was. Josh bent his head back as perspiration peppered the nape of his neck. The heat had dried his hair. "You might want to do something about the body in the pool outside Clearwater."

"I'll handle it," Tenuk replied.

He could feel Erin stiffen beside him.

"No other alerts?" he asked Tenuk as he took her hand, ran a thumb down her palm, trying to instill some sort of calm, of confidence.

Confidence? Calm?

What was he thinking? She'd just been shot at, had run for her life, been through a cave river and watched a man die. She was probably so shell-shocked she'd never be the same.

She squeezed his hand as if trying to convey the opposite.

"No. I've got the river covered. In fact, I've hired a couple of the men from the local tribes. They'll be better at it than any of us. I doubt this time anyone will be able to slip by. As far as the flights in are concerned, we've been monitoring that for a while." He nodded. "As I know you have. No other way except…" He glanced back to the quartz cliffs that punched jagged outlines in the crystalline sky.

"The back way, which means rock climbing and jungle trekking," Josh finished for him. "Not an improbability."

"You're right. We're on it."

"I hope to hell you are," Josh replied. "This was too close."

"You've got to get her out of here," Tenuk said. "That's the only way she's going to be safe."

"In the meantime, this can't happen again."

"It won't," Tenuk said grimly.

"That goes without saying," Josh replied and looked at Erin, trying to silently reassure her and thankful that she hadn't added her thoughts to the discussion. He wished she wasn't here, that she were someplace where danger was only a part of fictional entertainment. And conversely he was glad she was here, where he could see her and know she was safe. He wanted her physically by his side from here on in.

"You're all right?" he asked Erin again.

She looked from him to Tenuk, fear and hope in her eyes.

"Fine, for now. A little shook up."

"An understatement, I'd imagine," Tenuk put in.

"We'll get you out of here, Erin. Trust us."

She nodded. "I suppose I don't have much choice."

"A woman of common sense and logic." Tenuk's laugh fell flat. "The resort is clear," he said to Josh. "I suggest you keep her in your room until it's time to take off. I'll give you the signal."

"Same as before."

"Same." Tenuk smiled and winked at Erin.

She said nothing, neither acknowledging nor ignoring Tenuk's rather fresh gesture. Josh suspected that it was Tenuk's way of making Erin feel more comfortable in a situation that had to be anything but comfortable.

He put a hand on her shoulder in comfort and reassurance. They would talk more when Tenuk left, and he hoped the hand on her shoulder silently told her that.

He felt the tension in her and wished he could explain more than he planned to, enough to make her comfortable, less in the dark. So much of what he did was under the table. The bird whistles that Tenuk had used through their three-day stay here to alert him to her comings and goings once she was outside her room, the furtive communications with Wade, the arrangements to get her out of here. All were things he could not reveal.

"It will be okay. You'll see. I'm getting you out of here," Josh said as they headed for his room.

He felt her tense and realized his error.

She looked up at him with haunted eyes and she said nothing.

But the tension that seemed to strum from her said everything.

Out of here, no matter what he said before, meant home, to the States, to San Diego where it had all begun.

Chapter Nineteen

He opened the door and guided her in, his hand on the curve of her waist. She turned to look at him with resignation and, despite everything she'd just been through and heard, or maybe because of it, what he suspected was distrust.

"We'll wait here in my room for Tenuk to give us the all clear. I don't want you alone or at least out of sight." Tension rippled between them.

"I can't believe it. The river isn't safe. A boat trip… I thought…" She shivered and pushed a thread of hair from her brow. "That's how I meant to get out." She shook her head. "I never thought danger would come that way. I should have."

Her shoulders shook, and she wrapped her arms under her chest as if to self-comfort. It had been too much. She was a civilian, a grade-school teacher, unprepared for such trauma.

"The hit man, killer, whatever you want to call him, obviously thought the same. As Tenuk verified, that was the way he slipped in." His hand still rested on her waist as he tried to instill confidence in her, ease her jitters, and at a minimum, let her know that he was there for her in any way she needed him. He needed her to keep it together during these next hours. And if she could do that, he'd get her out of here, keep her safe.

But as before he was blindsided by the feel of her, by the heat that ran through his palm as he touched her and by the desire that her nearness aroused. He dropped his hand and closed the door.

"Have a seat," he offered, for he could see her fingers trembling as she tried to hold them rigid at her side.

She was destroying his equilibrium. He didn't do damsels in distress, not literally and not figuratively. He'd lifted many people out of sticky foreign jams but never an attractive woman whose curves had pressed up against him one too many times and whose body he couldn't help but notice.

He told himself that he couldn't think such thoughts. Attraction was dangerous in the field. She was the object of his rescue, nothing more. To think anything else endangered them both.

"You've been through hell, and I don't mean just today, Erin Kelley Argon," he said.

She ran a finger along the blind and then pulled the cord, closing off the outside world. "I don't suppose we should leave them open."

She turned to look at him with traces of fear still in her eyes, and he only wanted to fold her in his arms and never let her go.

"I think I need you to say it again," she whispered. "Who you are."

"Josh Sedovich, just like I said. CIA."

Her eyes were as blue as a clear winter day, and troubled. He closed the distance between them.

"Erin." His hands dropped to her shoulders. He imagined the silky skin beneath the thin cotton and instead pressed his lips to hers, pushing them open, tasting her.

A faint sweetness flirted with his tongue as he pulled her tight against his chest. Her lips were soft and yielding. Her tongue tentatively touched his as her body leaned into his.

Her palm skimmed almost flirtatiously against his forearm. The scent of something like jasmine seemed to waft from her. And all the adrenaline that had rushed through him earlier now settled in his groin. He bit back a groan and along with that the urge to bend her backward over his arm.

Instead, he pulled her closer, his hands slipping from her waist to cup her bottom, lush even through the rough cotton pants, and he drew her even closer as he dipped her back and his lips again claimed hers.

A soft moan escaped her, and his tongue plunged deeper, wanting to duplicate that somewhere else, knowing it was too soon. Her breasts pressed against him, warm, giving, suggesting so many other possibilities, and he only wanted to rip off the clothes that stood between them.

"How did you get hooked up with trash?" he breathed. It was a sentence that forced his mind to reality, an attempt to control his wayward body.

She went still.

Her silence seemed to echo between them. She pushed against his chest, taking a step back, her jaw set.

"Trash," she repeated. Her face was taut and almost expressionless. Her hand reached out, and she slapped him, the sound loud and cold in the room. The slap seemed to vibrate between them as they stood unmoving in a face-off of indecision on her part and of silent respect on his. She was like a deer on the highway, unsure if it should run or freeze, and it was his fault. He had made a beautiful moment ugly. A moment that had taken her away from the fear and panic she had so recently experienced had now been destroyed.

"I'm sorry. That was uncalled for," she said after a full minute went by during which neither of them moved.

His cheek stung but it was a minor assault considering everything she'd been through.

"Completely understandable. You've been through a lot. And…" Diplomacy, he reminded himself even as he voiced his thoughts.

She looked at him with eyes wide and troubled. He wanted to hold her, to stroke her, to… He took a step back. He wanted to do more than get her out of here and into the hands of the legal system. He wanted… He bit back the last of his thoughts. It didn't matter what he wanted. He couldn't have her, not any more than he'd had, and that had been a mistake.

"In your shoes I may have done the same."

"I doubt if you would have ever been in my shoes," she said softly.

It was a truth he couldn't disagree with. Instead, he said, "It's real, Erin. I mean who I am, why I'm here." Outside the afternoon was drifting to a close and the resort was quiet. He'd considered suggesting that they go to the dining room, but all things considered, he thought it would be best to remain here, quiet and out of sight until Wade arrived. They'd missed lunch. He'd notify Tenuk, get a meal brought over.

"You do this for a living. You're an expert." It was a redundant statement that he suspected she needed to say to grasp everything that had happened. She clenched the fist of her right hand before looking up at him. "My luck ran out, didn't it?"

He couldn't disagree with her there, not on either point.

If the Anarchists hadn't delayed, if their leader hadn't escaped capture for so many months, it would have been different. As it was, she'd had a reprieve. That aside, he had to admit she'd been good, the slip out of the States brilliant in her method of transportation. The rest, the access to another passport, was the luck of birth.

"We have a window, Erin. Like you heard, we'll be out of here tonight." He took her hand. "Are you hungry?"

"No, I…" She shook her head. "I'm not hungry, not in the least." She looked at him with eyes that were wide and pleading. "I can't go back, not to the States."

"You've got to get out of Mulu. What happened this afternoon will keep happening until they succeed." If it was possible, her face went even paler. He didn't need to mention the fact that the local authorities would be on this soon, too. He'd already staved them off, temporarily.

"Until they…"

She held up her hand. "No, Josh. Don't say it. I know. I wake up every morning knowing this could be my last." She shook her head. "I never thought it would come to this. That not only Daniel but Emma would be dead because of me."

"Not because of you," he said, although in a way what she said was true.

"No?" She looked up at him with pain in her eyes. "She befriended me, offered me a place to stay for a week, and I left her that damn note."

"She didn't send it on."

"You knew?"

"I found it when I went to the apartment. Mike never saw that note."

"It doesn't matter. She died because she knew me. And Daniel, too." Her voice seemed to crumble, break up as if she could stand no more. She folded her arms, wrapping them around her chest.

"Erin. It wasn't you. It's the Anarchists and those they hire."

"I shouldn't have run."

"You had no choice." He reached for her, pulling her to him. She was stiff in his arms. He knew why she had run, knew about Sarah, but he needed to hear it in her own words. For then he would know that he had her complete trust.

"I can't go back." She pulled away, her lips set. "No one else must die because of me."

"And to stay overseas would be worse. You're flirting with death. They'll go after you and eventually everyone you know."

Her face went pale. "No."

"Yes," he said firmly. "I'm sorry, Erin, but this just isn't about you. Not anymore."

"I can't go home," she said.

"We're going to Georgetown for now." There was a no-argument tone in his voice.

"Georgetown? You're kidding me. I… They…" She shook her head. "No."

"You have to, Erin. No one's looking in Georgetown. Not now. It's the safest landing place out of here. And it's temporary, but…" He glanced at the window as if there might be someone listening but really he only wanted to give her a moment to absorb the reality. "Georgetown is safe despite what happened. The man who tried to kill you there…" Again, he paused for effect. "He followed you here."

"He's dead," she whispered.

"He is, and like I said there are others after him. Better, more experienced, no fail rates."

She frowned, and her eyes flitted from him to the door. "That man you were speaking to here…"

"Tenuk."

"He's the concierge and yet…"

"Malaysian Special Forces. He and a few of his men have been on watch these last few days. We're in the clear for now, but I can't guarantee how long that might last. We've got no choice but to get you out of Mulu tonight."

"You're sure?"

"As sure as I can be," he said. He fingered the handle of his gun and watched as her eyes followed. "I'll protect you, Erin. That's why I'm here." He'd repeat that fact as many times as she needed it to be repeated. He knew what shock did to a person, and she'd been through more in the past hours than many people had in a lifetime.

She crossed her arms and then dropped them. Her eyes didn't have that sparkle, that edge that he was so used to. Instead, there was a look of resignation on her face.

"Erin, let's get you safe." He took her upper arms, felt the silken, well-toned flesh, looked into her eyes and said, "Georgetown is the least likely point of discovery." Return to the place you'd fled. He'd used the same tactic in other assignments.

"I don't have many options, do I?"

"Not at the moment. From Georgetown we'll get you out of Malaysia," he replied as he sat her gently on the edge of the bed.

She folded her arms as if that would offer some comfort to the overwhelming thought of what the future held. And he knew what she was thinking: a return to the States where she suspected that the danger still hadn't been mitigated. She was loyal and she would not expose her sister to danger. But now wasn't the time to reveal all that he knew, including where Sarah was at this moment.

She held up her hand. "Look, I'm still shaking, and you do this for a living?"

"It's not always so dramatic."

"I can't imagine worrying, the possibility that someone you love might die, that…" Her eyes glistened with unshed tears.

"You're not talking about me are you?" Josh asked as he traced his thumb along the corner of her eye and wiped away the tear.

"No." She shook her head. "My brother died doing what he loved—heli-skiing. We begged him to not go that day. And he did." Silence hung briefly between them. "It destroyed my mother. In and out of therapy… What he did, it was horrible that he died, but what that did to my mother… So unfair."

"Tragic," he agreed. "But no more unfair than running with shady men who end up having you leave your family behind and live a false life overseas. Is that fair to those who care about you?" She'd provided him with the appropriate time to finally dig under her skin, draw a bit of blood and hopefully expose the truth.

"It wasn't like that. You know that, don't you?"

He said nothing.

"I know what you're trying to do. And I hate it." Her laugh was dry, mirthless. "But we have time to waste, and I want to know about you. I like you and putting yourself in danger with every—" She stopped as if pondering. "What do they call it? Assignment?"

"Close enough. It's a thrill, I suppose, and a job. Maybe a bit of both and difficult to explain." And he wasn't sure why he was allowing the shift in topic except that knowing about him might make it safe for her to reveal more about herself. "Maybe that was too simplistic. I suppose, for me it's more about giving back to others what my parents never had—security. On a trip home to Czechoslovakia when I was five they were detained for months. My mother was never the same after, neither was my father. A loving relationship basically crumpled before my eyes and became instead, abusive. I didn't want that to happen to anyone else. I suppose that was my underlying motivator to do this—not the thrill." He turned away. "At least that's what I said going in. One year later my motivation changed completely. My mother was raped and murdered in a home invasion." His eyes narrowed and for a moment he looked away. "It could have been any house on the block. They chose hers." He swallowed heavily. "Fate."

"I'm sorry. I didn't realize."

"Enough of my past," he said. They had little time and he needed information. "When was the last time you heard from Mike Olesk?"

Erin started and her mouth tightened.

"What's wrong?"

She ran her hands down her upper arms as if that would ward off the chill.

"Tell me," Josh said as his arm went around her shoulders, drawing her against his side.

"If you're thinking that Mike had anything to do with this, with finding me, then you're wrong. Mike would never do that. Ever," she said as if for emphasis. "He was my father's friend. When we were younger, he was like an uncle. We lost touch after my father died. He worked in law enforcement. He knew how to keep quiet."

"And he wasn't around for a lot of years until you contacted him," Josh said. "But as an old family friend, you trusted him," he guessed.

He wondered if that trust had been misplaced. People had been turned for surprisingly small amounts of money, and the money in question here was much more than that. But for now it was only a suspicion like any other. "When did he contact you last, Erin?"

"I got an email from him after leaving Singapore. It said simply, King of Malaysia. You know, referring to King George II, who Georgetown was named for."

"Mike told you to come to Malaysia, to Georgetown?" It was a question that lacked the element of surprise. He had seen this coming. Did it mean Mike Olesk was involved? He couldn't rule it out.

"Mike had nothing to do with this, if that's what you're thinking." She faced him, her fists clenched. "He wanted me to be able to lie low for a while. He got me safely to Georgetown. And he was right. I was safe for a long time. He had nothing to do with any of it, not with Daniel or Emma." She shook her head, and tears filmed her eyes. "That was over two months ago that he contacted me. The last time I ever heard from him. The last…" Her voice broke up as emotion got the better of her.

This time he didn't try to comfort her, didn't put his arm around her. He instinctively knew that she needed space.

Two months for the Anarchists to find Mike, maybe a bit of time for them to come up with the right amount of money. It was possible, even probable. He remembered the shifty look of the older man's eyes, as if Mike were keeping a secret.

"It's okay. Trust me. I'll get you out of here." It was all he could say for now. The last thing he needed was for her to fall apart. But as he met Erin's troubled eyes, he realized that falling apart was not an option. Her eyes were filmed with tears but her shoulders were set in a stoic angle. She'd hold it together. He could count on that.

He ran his finger along her cheek, wiping a tear that escaped.

"Don't," he said thickly. "Don't cry. It's all going to work out."

She looked up at him and connected in a way that snaked hotly through him as he saw more trust in her eyes than anyone had given him in a long time. He leaned down and kissed her, his hand caressing her cheek, feeling her softness and yet sensing an iron core—an iron core that they'd need to see their way through.

Chapter Twenty

"You can't outrun them," Josh said as his hand rested on her forearm, strong and warm. A shiver ran through her. "You have to face this thing. It's the only way it will ever end."

She stood up and turned away from him, hating every word he said for it was the truth. "You know, don't you?"

"About what happened that night?" He walked over to the window, raised the blind with his forefinger and looked out. Then he went to the door, opened it and looked around. He came back and sat down beside her. "I was briefed before I left."

"Briefed," she murmured. "It all sounds so cold…so clinical."

He shrugged.

She knew he wouldn't disagree with her assessment. She suspected that it was his strong willpower that allowed him to put his emotions and personal judgments to the background, and allowed him to do this kind of work.

"They think you're a witness who will help pin a murder charge on the leader of one of the most influential biker gangs in the world. They assume, apparently, that your testimony is doubly important because it is also proof of what was already suspected—the gang's high-priced connections and funding out of Europe." He folded his arms, his six-foot-plus frame intimidating, she imagined, if you didn't know how much he cared. "While that's not exactly how it came down, and not quite your reason for running, I just can't see how you got involved with them. Was it the thrill? What drives a woman like you to fall in with a biker gang, especially one as notorious as the Anarchists?"

"It wasn't like that." She shook her head, ignoring the other implications.

He reached over and covered the back of her hand with his. "Tell me how it really happened. Not how it was reported." His voice was a low growl that sent a shiver down her spine.

She took a breath.

She needed him for now—to get out of Mulu. That was it. There was nothing else. After that they would part ways and she would flee—alone, as she had for the past five months. There was no other choice. Fear ran through her about what he wasn't telling her. Did he know about Sarah? He wasn't saying, and she couldn't ask without arousing his curiosity. She couldn't take the chance and she couldn't ask the question.

Her mind went to that night as it had done over and over again during the months since it had happened.

She remembered odd things about that spring evening, the buzz of a fly that had somehow gotten into the car. The rich smell of living things in full bloom overlaid by the sweet, rather wistful scent of lilac. It was festival time and Cinco de Mayo was only a week away.

She remembered the house, a stately two-story Spanish Colonial set on ten acres just outside San Diego. She'd gone there knowing her boyfriend Steven would be there. Unfortunately, Sarah had insisted she should come along. Sarah, who had been almost four months pregnant.

"The smell of blood," she whispered. "It was horrible. I'll never forget…"

"Why didn't you report it?" Josh asked, breaking into her thoughts.

She looked at him, caught in her memories, and it took a second to bring herself to the present and a question she suspected would be difficult for an outsider to understand. She took a breath. "Steven, he wasn't there like he promised and then he showed up outside as I was leaving, almost out of nowhere. Told me it was unfortunate and tragic and that he didn't want me involved. He said that he'd report it to the police immediately, tell them that he'd stumbled on it. Not mention my name."

"And you believed him?"

"I wouldn't have in other circumstances but then— well, it was traumatic. I only wanted to go home where it was safe." She shook her head. "At least where I thought it was safe."

"Let me guess. He didn't report it?"

"I didn't see Steven again after that day."

"And you didn't file your report, either?"

"No, by the time I realized that Steven hadn't, I knew who had died and what I'd seen. I identified the men from pictures on the news report and after that I spoke to Mike."

She thought of all that had transpired what seemed a lifetime ago. It had all happened so quickly. One day she had been fielding teaching gigs as a substitute teacher in San Diego and the next minute she had been running for her life. Mike was the only person she trusted with what she saw, or rather, what Sarah had seen. Even with him she hadn't told him the truth of who was the witness. Even then she had tried to protect Sarah. Mike had laid out her options. He had briefed her on how to disappear.

He'd given her tips, and she'd cobbled the details together herself. But it had been Mike who had guided her. And with no experience in such things, she had taken his advice and began to consider the worst possibility she could imagine. Leaving her home and running.

"YOU'RE NOT HOW I imagined you'd be," Josh said.

"How did you imagine me?" Erin asked. Her heart thumped a little extra beat as she anticipated what he might say, how he had thought of her. Worse, how he might think of her now. Steven and all that he had drawn her into had not been her best moment.

He paced the room and then stopped. "It isn't a flattering picture, Erin. I have to say that."

"I imagine it's not," she said quietly. "To say my ex-boyfriend was a mistake is an understatement."

He nodded. "After reading the report I thought you might be a bit ditzy but intelligent. Perpetually drawn to the allure of adventure, to the bad boy. Textbook. And after I spoke to Mike, well, I..."

Her stomach clenched at the thought of that.

"He said you were naive. That you had first real boyfriend syndrome. Finished school too young and were sheltered, spoiled even."

"He said all that?" The enormity of what Josh was saying was too much to take in. And oddly it was Josh's word she trusted. Mike, the old friend of her father's, one of the last few reminders of her father—to think he had said those things was a breach of trust, and a smackdown she'd never seen coming.

She stood up, went to the window and then turned away, too disheartened to lift the blind or look out. "I was never any of that."

"Never?"

She whirled around. "You know nothing about me," she said through clenched teeth, the memories fresh. She looked at him and saw compassion flirting in the depths of his eyes. She swallowed, cleared her throat and said, "And yet you assume everything."

"Then enlighten me."

"I don't know if I can."

"Trust me," he said softly.

She took a breath. "Steven never wore the colors or dressed like a biker, at least when he was with me. Not until that night." She shook her head. "Of course, I knew before that, that something wasn't right, that Steven wasn't just a regular guy. I'd seen his friends, heard some of their talk and put some of it together. I knew he was a biker. I just didn't know he was an Anarchist."

"Tell me about it." His voice was gruff with a raw edge. "About that night. The night that Antonio Enrique died." Antonio Enrique. The Spanish billionaire was proof of the Anarchists' ties to old money and the European funding connection. And his death was what would take the leader of the Anarchists down—for murder.

She gripped the windowsill as she turned away from him. "I planned to break up with Steven. I wanted nothing to do with him or the gang. But..." She leaned one hip against the sill, her face turned sideways to him. "I would have broken up anyway if Steven had a normal career. He wasn't my type of guy."

"Steven Decker," Josh mused. "Arrested three weeks ago attempting to cross the Mexican border near Tijuana. Drug running." There was nothing but disdain in his voice. "I suspect there may be other charges pending."

The news shocked her but emotionally she felt nothing. She'd never loved him and the thought of who he was and what she'd been to him made her sick. But arrested? She couldn't imagine the free-spirited man she'd known behind bars. She didn't want to imagine any of it. She wanted to hit Rewind.

"It was inevitable. What puzzles me was what you saw in him." He frowned as he looked at her. "You're into bad-boy types?"

She shook her head, and her hair slapped across one cheek. "No. God, no. Like I said, I didn't know that was what he was. I met him at a movie. Actually, I spilled my popcorn into his lap. I thought there was nothing bad about him."

"A movie?"

"You don't believe me?"

"Unfortunately, I do."

"Steven." She shook her head. "He didn't even like to be called Steve. He had a motorcycle, a Harley, but that's no different than a thousand other bikers in California. The only thing that was strange is that I never saw where he lived. He always picked me up, and we would go different places." There was a look on her face that almost made him want to believe her, almost. "I didn't know." She hesitated. "I should have."

"But at some point you found out," he encouraged. "I read the report but a report is nothing more than a dry collection of facts. And…"

She pushed a strand of hair from her face, slipping it behind her ear. "You've been briefed, as you call it. So I suspect you know most of it already."

"I do." He nodded. "But I'd like if you'd tell me yourself."

And she did, starting with their first date to that fateful night.

"It was horrible. I didn't see much. I heard arguing and

I saw their faces briefly." She swallowed, hating the lies she'd told, hating all of it.

"So how did you put it all together?"

"Like I said, a news report that night and then…"

"That's not how it came down, is it?" he said with a hard edge in his voice.

She looked up at him and saw something in his eyes, something that frightened her. "No." She shook her head. "That's exactly how it happened."

This time she couldn't look at him for he would see the fright in her eyes.

"You weren't alone, were you?" He paused and silence filled the room. "There's a witness to that murder, but it wasn't you. Was it, Erin?"

"What do you mean?"

"You're protecting someone. I hoped you would tell me who—voluntarily."

Silence dragged between them as her eyes averted his and dodged to the gleaming wooden floor.

"It's Sarah, isn't it? Your sister."

She stood paralyzed, her hand gripping the sill.

"I know you didn't witness that murder. That you're protecting Sarah, but what I don't know is why."

"Is she…" Her voice was choked.

"She's safe. She's in protective custody. They won't get her. Either her or, what was the damn cat's name?"

"Edgar." Relief flooded her voice. Was he telling her the truth? What reason did he have to lie? "Sarah's safe?"

"Protected 24/7 by our best."

"How long have you known…has the CIA known?"

"FBI, you mean. It was their gig until you stepped off American soil. That's where I came in."

Her knees threatened to give out and she had to consciously breathe to regain control.

"Are you okay?" Josh asked as his hand rested gently on her shoulder. The heat of it seemed to burn through the light cotton material and she wanted to turn and lean closer into his arms, into the comfort of his embrace. But now wasn't the time.

"How did you find her?"

"I don't know the details of that," Josh said. "The only detail I'm concerned about right now is you." There was an undercurrent in his voice that sent a tremor through her. "Tell me what really happened."

She shook her head. It was all so difficult.

He drew her into his arms.

"I care about you, Erin. More than I should. I wouldn't lie to you about Sarah. I know she's important to you."

She looked at him and met the truth in his eyes.

She took in a breath and as he held her she told him what had happened that day. Her voice was steady but she thought that it might only be his arms around her that held her up.

"Sarah heard scuffling and like a fool she went in. And that's when the murder happened. She saw the leader of the Anarchists turn, saw his face in a mirror and, thank God, he didn't see her."

"Giving you the perfect opportunity to run in her place," Josh said. "Very brave, but…"

"Stupid."

"No, not that," Josh said quietly and drew a strand of hair from her face.

She looked up at him and felt hope that maybe with him she could face anything, including the Anarchists.

Together.

She pulled away from him and took a step back.

She tried to reel in her emotions, corral them, but it was impossible. In three days she had done the unfathomable. In the wrong time and place and with the wrong man, worse, one she knew little about, she had done the unthinkable.

It couldn't be, but no amount of wishing made it go away.

She'd fallen in love.

Chapter Twenty-One

Erin drew in a long breath. It seemed as though her knees wouldn't hold her, and she found herself again in his arms. She should pull away. She knew that as well as she knew that she didn't have the will to combat what might follow.

"It's going to be all right. I've got you."

She turned her face into his shoulder as pent-up emotion, relief, tension, all of it seemed to flood through her. She wasn't sure she could have stood without the support of his arm around her waist.

"Sarah's safe?" She shivered as she looked at him. She so wanted to believe that it was true, but it seemed impossible. It had been too long coming, yet, this man had risked his life and saved them both, and he was willing to put his life on the line again.

"She's well taken care of. She couldn't be safer. So tell me," he said. "Why didn't you file a report, despite what Steve Decker said?"

"I wanted to, but Sarah was adamant that we shouldn't. She told me she'd heard begging, that the victim…" She swallowed hard. "Was begging for his life. She saw chaps and leathers, too. Bikers. She was sure of it. But what she was also sure of after watching a news report later that night was that she'd watched the leader of the Anarchists murder someone." She shook her head. "I mean the Anarchists, well, they terrified me, especially after I spoke to Mike." She looked up at him. "They won't stop looking." It wasn't a question but a fact that she had feared through her entire flight.

"And Steven?"

She shook her head. "He was there, like I said. He showed up as I was leaving the house."

"Explains why the Anarchists went after you."

She shook her head. "I never wanted to believe that of him, but who else could it have been? And Mike, he confirmed it." She took a breath. "Thank God he never saw Sarah."

"So he was saving his own skin."

"I suppose so. Saved me the breakup speech." She smiled shakily.

"Circumstances worked against you," he said.

"Enough of Steven. How do we stop them?"

"At this point, we don't. Specifically, you don't," he said. "That's why you need me."

"Oh, God." She seemed to fold into herself, her heart beating too loud, too fast. Everything seeming so futile.

His arms were tight around her, and she shuddered.

"You're going to make it. I promise. But it's time to go home."

"Home," she murmured as his lips met hers, and for the first time it felt as though it could be a possibility as her arms went around his neck. Her breasts pressed tight against the muscled ribbing of his chest. All of it felt so right even when the timing was so completely wrong, even when he was wrong. The wrong man. She couldn't imagine the chances he took, the day-to-day complications of what he did for a living. It was incomprehensible. But more incomprehensible were her feelings for him. She shouldn't have them. She didn't know him.

"You're safe, baby," he said against her lips as she wrapped her arms around his neck.

She wanted to melt into him, and for a moment what awaited them outside this resort was forgotten. All the doubts, the possibilities of the future melted into the present. There was only this man, this moment and a relief so intense that as it shifted into passion, everything seemed to implode.

His hand ran down the light cotton material of her blouse, slipped beneath the hem. Skin on skin, his hand warm and rough. She wanted that hand there. She wanted more. She...

"Josh..."

She slipped free. It wasn't that easy. It couldn't be. She'd been running too long. She moved a few steps away as if in distance there would be answers, salvation, something.

His hands were on her shoulders, solid and comforting and sensual, even though it was nothing more than the touch of a hand through cloth.

He pulled her close, her derriere cupped against his thighs.

He ran his hand along her side, curving at her waist and settled it on her hip.

"I haven't wanted a woman like I want you in a long time," he whispered, his breath hot and scintillating against her ear. She shivered against him, against the hardness that pressed against her and called for her to turn and offer him everything she had. She stayed with her back to him and let his hands go where they would.

His hand circled her belly and slid upward. Her blouse slipped off one shoulder. The buttons of her blouse were undone. A warm hand covered her naked breast and she didn't know how they had gotten to this point, except

that she wanted to turn in to him and was held firmly
against his hips, at his mercy, as his fingers toyed with
her nipples and as her breathing came just a little hotter
and just a little faster.

She barely noticed as her blouse fell to the ground,
landing in a puddle at her ankles. His hands dropped
lower, to the curve of her waist, her hips, the V between
her legs, holding her there, making her arch and want to
turn and reach for him.

"Josh."

Behind them a breeze lifted the canvas blind, rustling
in the tight heat that seemed to settle around them.

She hesitated as everything that had happened and that
she had yet to face slipped to the background and passion
threatened to consume her.

He nuzzled her earlobe, the soft caress making her
shudder even as she shook her head.

"I want you," she murmured as her fingers ran tentatively down the hard muscle of his broad back. Her hand
dropped.

"There can never be anything between us, Josh. This
is just an illusion, a place where I should never be and a
place where you always are. A dangerous place."

His hand stilled between her legs as she wept, wanting him.

"You're too risky."

He ran a thumb over her nipple.

Pinpoints of pleasure ran through her. "Men like
you…"

She pulled away from him before it was too late, before passion swept reason out of reach.

"And who or what, exactly, are men like me?"

She picked up her blouse and pulled it on. She took her

time gathering her disjointed thoughts, breathing slowly and getting her traitorous body under control.

She did up the last button before meeting his eyes.

"Men who thrive on adrenaline, on fast-paced lives and equally fast-paced relationships. Men who will never own a home and mow a front lawn." She looked away, one hand working through the fingers of another and then she looked at him, seeing the truth in his eyes.

"Erin…"

"It's true, isn't it? I bet you don't even have a pet or a neighbor you know or…"

"An RV just outside of Tampa," he said and walked to the window. He stood there for a long moment, his dark hair curling over his collar, his shoulders broad and tapering to slim hips.

He was everything she wanted in a man, yet everything she didn't. He was danger, and he was compassion. She'd never seen that in any man.

"A camping trailer?" She smiled and shook her head. "Wouldn't an apartment work better?"

"It's a little bigger than that. And as far as portability, well, I liked the allure of the open road at the time I bought it. As it is, it's been in an RV park just outside Tampa for the last five years." He leaned one hip against the windowsill. "I've gotten used to the small space and knowing that if I feel like it I can move it at any time." He cleared his throat and pushed away from the sill. "Except I've never felt like it. Like moving."

"But you're not a stay-at-home kind of guy?"

"Not lately," he admitted. "I'm not home a lot, but I am handy, if that helps. At least my friends think so."

"Handy?"

"I spent the last vacation plumbing a friend's bathroom." He ran a hand through his hair. "Seems like years ago."

He smiled at her and it seemed odd, the smile and even the conversation, considering what they had just gone through and where they'd just been.

"I know, hard to believe."

"It is," she replied. The image of him raising that gun, of the man…falling and… She closed her eyes. She couldn't think of it. It was hard, even after seeing him in action, to think that the gentle, unassuming man she had met was capable of those things or worse. And if he weren't capable of those things, it was even harder to face the other truth, that she would now be dead.

"It's all been too much. I'm sorry," he said and his voice had a gruff edge. "I would change all of this if I could."

"How do you do this day in and day out one assignment after another?"

He shrugged. "I suppose I was drawn to it after spending my youth traveling the globe. I left home after two years of college and spent a couple of years traveling. And, of course, what happened to my family when they were detained."

She digested all of that. "I can't even begin to imagine. Does it fulfill you?"

"Some days," he said honestly. "And other days I'm not sure if I shouldn't be doing something else."

"But you didn't finish college?"

"One day I may finish. In the meantime, life has been my university."

"A rather tough way to get an education." She laced her fingers together.

"Erin." His voice was gruff, and then she was in his arms and he was holding her and it felt so good, so safe.

The scent of him was warm with the clean scent of the outdoors. His chest was solid against her, comforting.

The chirp of a jungle insect seemed to knife through the room, and Erin shuddered, remembering who and what might be out there, maybe not nearby, not yet... but soon.

"I'm sorry you had to see any of that," he said.

"Don't be," she replied. "You saved my life."

"Just part of the job," he said as he strode across the room, putting distance between them. A whistle rather like the call of a bird had Josh opening the door. She watched as he nodded to someone she couldn't see. He opened the door wider, and Tenuk stood a few feet back from the doorway, looking serious.

"I'm going with Tenuk—five minutes. I won't be out of sight of the room."

"You want me to stay here...alone?"

He stepped back and placed his hands on her shoulders. "It'll be all right. We're close to getting you the hell out of here."

Hell, she thought. That was what she had been through and as she met the sincerity in his eyes she realized, that hell might be what she would be facing when all this was over.

When she went home, to Sarah, to the safe house.

When she was home—without him.

Chapter Twenty-Two

Early evening, Wednesday, October 14

"Just heard from Wade," Tenuk said. "Georgetown is out of the question."

"Why?" Josh snapped.

"Wade would be here in under an hour, but he's reported a major foul up at the airport. A crash has Georgetown's runways closed and emergency measures in place. I suspect it won't be much longer before Wade gets around that, but he's not going to be here as scheduled."

"How soon?"

"Another couple of hours." Tenuk shrugged and handed Josh a small slip of paper. "Here's the numbers of the plane. Don't ask me how Wade got them before he got on the plane. Or for that matter how he contacted me. Only thing you need to know is that's our plane. Be sure to destroy this in the usual manner." Josh nodded. He'd chewed and swallowed more than his share of paper.

IT WAS NEAR nine o'clock before they heard the buzz of a small plane, an Otter, similar to the ones the resort used. Josh went outside, and Erin could see from the window as he looked upward.

"It's time to get out," he said, leaving the door open behind him.

Erin hesitated.

It was the moment of truth, when she gave him her trust not just in this moment but all of it going forward. It was a lot to ask considering everything that had gone before, how long she'd depended solely on herself. She hesitated, taking in his sun-burnished good looks, the cap and tourist T-shirt gone. The plain black T-shirt defined his flat belly, defined his muscle—reminded her that he was all man.

Too much man.

Too much risk.

"Erin." His voice broke into her thoughts, his hand warm yet oddly commanding on her forearm. "This is it. The plane is here. Stay close. It should be clear but…"

His hand slid from her forearm as he held out his hand. "We're going to have to hurry."

Despite her thoughts she hesitated only briefly, and as she did the impact of it all whirled through her mind. This was life changing, epic, and it would affect both her and Sarah. What if she were wrong?

"Move," he said, and his tone suggested that there was no possibility of hesitation.

His grip went back to her arm as he propelled her forward. "The next man destined to try to take you out is on his way. He was seen up river not that long ago. Remember what I told you earlier? More deadly than anyone who has tracked you before."

She swallowed heavily, digesting that information, trying to stay calm.

Outside, they hurried along the wooden pathway. She could sense Josh's tension in the tight grip he had on her hand. He nodded at a maid who moved lightly along the boardwalk, a bag of cleaning supplies over her arm. She was the only person they met on their walk to the tarmac. As they left the wooden walk it almost seemed like the verdant green jungle had taken on an ugliness that was foreign, where once, or maybe in another time and place, it had been beautiful.

Her imagination was in overdrive.

She took a breath. The jungle seemed to be the same, rich and thick, full of the calls of the birds. But the rustling in the brush no longer signified something amazing, possibly camera worthy like wildlife. Instead, it felt as if it was a trap that housed a game of life and death.

The grip on her hand was so tight she could feel the bones shift.

"Josh," she protested.

The jungle seemed to breathe around them, the darkness providing another layer, one of danger. There was nothing to see but thick shadows. Something shrieked deep in the jungle's depths and she jumped as a shiver ran across her spine. Whoever the next tracker was he could be in the jungle, and they would never know until it was too late.

They stepped off the walkway heading for the tarmac.

They were out in the open, exposed. Her palms were damp, and a knot in the pit of her stomach that combined with the sour taste in her mouth made her fight against the urge to throw up.

She looked ahead. The plane was on the runway, the shadow of the pilot in the cockpit and the propellers going. The plane was ready to take off.

Time was running out. She could feel it in the short gasps of breath, in the pounding of her heart, in the sweat that slicked her palm against his.

It had been so few hours since they'd made a run for their lives through the cave and now it threatened to begin again.

Erin gasped for breath and saw the door to the plane open, a weathered-looking, blond-haired man flagging them in a one-armed wave.

"Hurry." Josh's command was overlaid with urgency as he moved faster and for a second she was unable to keep up and then she stumbled.

Josh pulled her to her feet, quickly, easily and with no words of concern. There was no time.

The pilot was out of the plane, opening the door and waiting for them to get in.

"Josh. King of the grand exit," he said. "Good to see you, man."

"Wade. Good to get the hell out of here," Josh said as he helped Erin in.

The interior of the plane had a heavy, musty odor as if it had been in the jungle too long. She pushed a canvas tarp aside and crawled into the farthest seat from the door. She looked out the window, but there was little to see as it was smeared and streaked with what looked like dirt. She clenched her hand, her nails biting into her palm and held back the urge to ask questions.

Josh and Wade were settling themselves in and before long the plane was taxiing down the runway, and they were off.

"Where to after Georgetown?" she asked.

"Georgetown? Not in this plane, sweetheart." Wade turned around and smiled at her.

He looked at Josh. "You heard?"

"Tenuk told me. Anything else?"

"What?" Erin's heart thumped and her mouth went

dry. They had agreed to Georgetown. Not quite agreed, she admitted to herself, but she'd been comfortable with that option. Josh had made her comfortable with it and now he was changing it. She looked at Josh, demanding an answer as her eyes clashed with his. What else had Tenuk told him that she hadn't heard?

"Plane crash on the main runway. Officials are all over the area and the city is crawling with overhyped media. We've got to take you to a safe zone for now." Josh looked back, his concern evident as his eyes searched hers. "I'm sorry, Erin. Things are moving too fast, and I didn't get a chance to tell you."

But even as he apologized her mind was going back to that one word. *Safe*, the word that kept coming up, but looking at Josh and hearing the diversion, she was beginning to feel less than safe.

"What's the change? Tenuk didn't know what you had in mind," Josh asked with confidence in his tone that eased Erin's mind at the thought of a diversion.

"Pulau, Langkawi," Wade said. "Honeymooners island. Trite but effective."

Josh nodded. "How long?"

"We'll get another plane in by tomorrow afternoon to get you out."

"Have you been in contact with Vern?"

Erin pushed her hands against her belly as the plane lifted into the air. Her stomach seemed to drop with the increase in altitude. She didn't feel comfortable. She didn't like this, not knowing Wade, not knowing about the conversation with Tenuk and realizing that there was a lot that Josh might be doing that she wasn't aware of. Suddenly trust seemed like a shaky position to be in. She was running blind—trusting that he would save her. She didn't like it.

He looked back at her with a reassuring smile. "Vern is who I report to. The one who got me into this. Wade here…"

"Private contractor," Wade said as the plane banked into a turn.

"Give or take. A wild card who works for the CIA."

"You blew my cover," Wade complained.

It was a brief moment of lightheartedness in the midst of a black unreality.

"It'll be okay, babe," Josh murmured under his breath.

In her heart that was all she wanted, to rewind the mess that her life had become and to have it all boil down to a word so simple.

Babe.

BRIEFLY SHE CLOSED her eyes as if that would return her equilibrium and establish a more normal reality. She was on the run and this time she was no longer in control. Truthfully, she hadn't been in control for a while, maybe since she'd first laid eyes on Josh. She shivered as Josh turned and his hand settled on her lower arm.

"Despite how this looks, it will be okay." But his voice was grim.

"How can you be so sure that I couldn't have carried on without you?" She looked straight ahead, her eyes averted, her body almost vibrating with tension.

It was an outrageous thing to say considering everything that had happened. She would have been dead in Clearwater Cave or even before. She shuddered, not knowing what had pushed her to say such a thing.

He had rescued her. They both knew that.

"For one, you can't stay on the run anymore. It's only a matter of time before they'd take you to ground. And two, the FBI will protect you. You'll be safe with them."

She shifted back, against the wall of the plane as if that would offer any protection. Despite everything that had happened, somehow she still harbored doubt.

Fear ran through her. No matter what had come before, she'd made the wrong decision. Despite what she had said, despite trust, despite everything, she couldn't go home. Ever.

"You'll be safe. We'll keep you safe," Josh said.

She shivered.

"There isn't a choice." His gaze was solid and confident. "I hate to say this but…"

"Say it, Josh," she said and she fisted her hand as if that would protect her in some way against what was to come.

"You're in our custody whether you like it or not."

She'd known that. He'd as much as said it an hour ago, but she'd known it before that. It was the inevitable cost of life, her life. She'd accomplished the most important thing. Sarah was safe. There was a point where she had to trust, where she couldn't run anymore, not by herself—this was the point where she faced it all.

"Where do we go from Langkawi?" Her heart seemed to stop in her chest at the thought of the answer. She knew what he would say, where he was taking her. He'd told her, yet she had to ask again and again, as if that would make it palatable. As if by hearing the word she could imagine it as the place before she had run. A part of her past where there was nothing dark and deadly awaiting, where the risk had been mitigated. She wanted to believe that in the worst way.

"Home," Josh replied. "You know without me saying it again. There isn't any other choice."

Her stomach tightened at the thought, even though there was also a rush of jubilation at the idea of seeing her family again. But then that wouldn't happen, she'd be in a safe house along with her sister and as Josh had stated, not the same house, either. She'd be there until the trial was over and a conviction took place. And if a conviction didn't take place... It didn't bear thinking about.

Fear sliced through her with icy discomfort and she took a breath as she looked at him. She could see the jut of his jaw, the firm line of his lips and the determination in his eye. And something changed for her looking at him like that, strong, yet so vulnerable. He would always do what was right, no matter the cost. Her heart did a small thump as she realized how close she was to saying yes to everything he might offer, yet he had offered her nothing except returning her safely home.

Home.

In another time, another place—another way, it would have been everything.

"I'll keep you safe," he repeated.

His words were reassuring, and they shifted the paradigm of reality. They made everything real and right. How had it happened in such a short time, that she had fallen for him, fallen for the wrong man, in the wrong place? Wrong in every way. The risk her brother had taken was small in comparison to what this man did for a living. She couldn't risk it. She couldn't... But there was no stopping it. She loved him. She'd already admitted that, to herself, anyway.

"No worries, Erin. You're in good hands," Wade put in. "I've worked with this guy for half a decade now. There isn't any better. Except *moi*."

"Bastard, fishing for favors again," Josh said, but with a light edge in his voice.

She looked from one to the other, but already her thoughts were moving ahead. What to do when she got to Langkawi? He'd said she was in custody. Did she trust him? Could she? Were there any other options? She was so conflicted—trusting on one hand, distrustful on the other. Fear was the only emotion that seemed constant.

"If you run you'll jeopardize everything, not just yourself, but Sarah, too," he whispered as he leaned back to look at her. "You're going to make it. I promise. It's time to go home."

Her heart seemed to stop.

She looked at Josh. Now he was talking to Wade. They were speaking in undertones, and she could hear none of what was being said over the roar of the engine. She leaned forward, and Josh turned.

"You're all right?"

"Fine."

Her ears clogged as twenty minutes later they began their descent. And for the rest of their time in the air little had been spoken.

Another five minutes, maybe ten, and they stood alone on the tarmac, Wade and the plane gone.

"You'll be fine, babe." Josh leaned over and kissed her.

She took a step back. She wasn't too sure she wanted him or any of his romantic overtures. Not now. Not ever. They—couldn't be.

She spun around, away from him. She didn't need her thoughts full of anything but keeping out of reach of the Anarchists. She didn't need her thoughts full of him.

A small Malay man in a *longyi* that had a brown-and-white tie-dyed look to it came up to them, maneuvering easily in the long cotton wrap, his plastic flip-flops snapping against the pavement. He spoke to Josh with words that Erin didn't understand and that only upped her nervousness. Somehow those moments on the plane had seemed safe and now on the ground it was as if the danger breathed around her. Her nails bit into her palms as she looked at the black stretch of pavement lit by the runway lights. In the distance she could hear the waves crashing rhythmically onto the shore.

An island. She wasn't sure what Mike would say about that. She wished she could speak to him. She suspected he wouldn't like it. But Mike may have betrayed her…

It didn't bear thinking about.

She had to trust.

Josh.

He was still speaking words she didn't understand. They were words that would affect her future. She didn't take her eyes off him, as if that would change whatever was being decided. Josh nodded and the two men parted.

Josh came over. "We're here overnight. Pickup is arranged, as Wade said, tomorrow afternoon."

"It's safe?" It was a ridiculous question. Obviously it was safe. They wouldn't be here if it weren't.

He nodded. "For now we're a honeymooning couple. Enjoying sights, spending too much time indoors with…" He looked at her and winked. "With each other."

She crossed her arms.

"Kidding." He touched her elbow. "Look, I'm sorry. I was trying to lighten the mood just a bit. You can relax, at least for now."

"It's the *for now* that I'm worried about."

"Don't. That's why I'm here." His arm curved around her waist.

"We have no luggage."

He turned her around and there, sitting on the tarmac, were two dusty blue, hard-shelled suitcases that hadn't been there before.

"Unbelievable." She looked at Josh as a second thought came to mind. "Now where?"

"A cab to the nearest hotel, which is just around the

bend." He released his hold on her waist. "And a cab, my love, is right over there."

She turned but for a moment her eye caught on the lush greenery that was highlighted faintly in the artificial light and reflected the jungle that was so tight and thick that it seemed to choke her as it sprawled around them. Something screeched, and what sounded like a scream followed.

She jumped and muffled a shriek with a hand over her mouth. "I'm sorry. I just… I've never heard anything like it."

"Monkey. The island is full of them," Josh said as he picked up both suitcases.

"Let me carry—" she began, determined to be of some help.

"What kind of husband would I be if our honeymoon started out with you carrying the bags?" he asked with a small smile.

Her smile reflected his. "Not great, I suppose." She looked across the tarmac to the cab. "Okay then." She took a breath and stood tall. It would take all her focus to appear normal. A few minutes later she was wrestling with the sliding door of the van.

Josh reached over her shoulder. "Let me," he said as the door slid open in an uneven jerk. Erin got in and Josh threw in the bags. The driver grunted once, said something that she couldn't understand as Josh closed the door with a slam.

The ten-minute cab ride was silent. The driver's speed and maneuvering of the dated van that served as a cab was painfully slow. They passed only one other vehicle. It was all that broke the drive except for the vehicle's headlights and the lights from the resorts that offered peeks of the endless stretches of jungle on the inland side and the views of the ocean that stretched out beyond them on the left. If this had been any other time, if this were a normal vacation, if they had been a normal couple—it would have been ideal.

She looked at Josh, his face tense and alert, his classic good looks underscored by the courage and integrity he'd already shown her. He was a man who worked in the trenches and put his life on the line every day. He was the man who said he could save her after five months on the road when she thought that no one could.

The cab pulled into a graveled lane where a yard light revealed a low-slung building that was cloaked in weathered pink siding. A sign announced the resort's name in a slight right-handed list. To the left and about a hundred feet away, edging toward the nearby ocean, another yard light revealed a two-story, milk-white structure with five rooms up and another five down and stairs leading up to individual units. There was no one in sight. Early fall was the slowest season and this slightly run-down affair would not be a tourist's first choice.

"This is it?" she asked, though it really didn't matter. She hopped out behind him, watched as he spoke briefly to a short, balding man and then reached for their suitcases.

In minutes the door to their room was open, the keys were in Josh's hands and they were alone.

The room was desperately tiny. At first she wasn't sure how they and their bags would fit. Josh dropped their suitcases between two small, legless beds that were really only a pair of mattresses on the floor. Outside, there was a little veranda, enough room for the white plastic chair and the pot of dying flowers that now occupied it. A flight of stairs led to a path that the owner said went through low-lying brush and over to the beach. Even in the dark it was clear this location was idyllic. Had they been honeymooners, she could imagine appreciating it despite the accommodation's rustic edge.

"Romantic enough for you, love?"

"Cut it out," she demanded. Considering everything, she wasn't in the mood for teasing. "In another life this room would have been Flintstones funny. Unfortunately, now not so much." She pressed a forefinger to her temple, hoping to ward off another headache.

"This has been hard on you."

"You think?" she said and immediately recanted. "I'm sorry."

"Don't apologize for what you can't help."

"All right, I won't." She plunked down on the bed, sitting cross-legged only inches above the floor. "So what now?"

"We spend tonight here and then we head to the Malaysian mainland by small plane tomorrow afternoon."

"Back to our place of origin?"

"Not quite. We head to Kuala Lumpur and from there it's only a matter of a couple of stops and you're home." He shrugged. "I didn't plan this segment. Wade did. He claims with a little help from Vern. Considering the foul-up in Georgetown, this segment makes sense."

"Vern?" she asked, wanting to know more than the little he'd told her on the plane.

"The man who gave me this assignment. He's safely stateside. But he's who I report to when this is all done."

"A boss?"

"More or less."

She pinched her bottom lip with her thumb and forefinger as she thought about the logistics of everything.

"Stop it. Quit thinking so much," he said as he sat down beside her.

"We're safe here?" It was a moot point, but somehow

the question made it real, made the thought of safety something she could entertain.

"I think so." He put a hand on her thigh.

"Think?" She leaned closer into him, as it felt safer with him near.

"Nothing is guaranteed. But it's the option we thought safest."

Safest, she thought looking at him, feeling herself falling for the lure of his warm cinnamon eyes, breathing in the scent that was uniquely him—fresh air and something that smelled vaguely like pine—and feeling on edge and uncomfortable and only wanting…

She couldn't admit what she wanted.

He wasn't safe.

They weren't safe.

Nothing could ever be safe again.

Chapter Twenty-Three

"I don't know how you do this," Erin said. "This kind of assignment over and over. This kind of danger." She took a breath. "That's what I am, right? An assignment." She stood up. She rubbed her palms, as if the friction would ease her thoughts.

"I won't lie to you. That's what you were in the beginning," he admitted. "No more." He took her hand, pulling her down on the edge of the bed. The room was so tiny that a chair wouldn't fit now that their suitcases had been set down.

"I don't know what will happen when this is over, Erin, but I care for you. More than I should—more than I ever have before."

"I'm not sure how to take that," she said with a glimmer of a smile and wiped her eyes with the back of her hand. "But I'm glad you're here. Without you I wouldn't have made it."

He nodded. There was no need to say anything. There was more truth in what she said than she might ever know.

She turned to face him, her lips still quivering, and he cupped her face between his hands and kissed her. He could taste the salt of her tears between them, slicking his lips. His tongue caressed her lips as it ran along them devouring her tears and then devouring her. He ran his hand along the sleek skin of her neck, resting where he could feel the distant and rapid beat of her heart.

She was so much more than an assignment. She'd been more almost from the beginning. But what he felt for her could be dangerous, especially as they danced one step ahead of danger. They couldn't afford any distraction or any hesitation.

He sat back, his hand on her shoulder, his thumb caressing her collarbone. "I'll get you out of here, Erin, but you can't hesitate, question me—ever. That's important. Promise me that. No hesitation ever again, not now that you know who I am and why I'm here."

"I…"

"Hesitation can be lethal," he said grimly. "The Anarchists have a bounty on your head. Ten million dollars."

"Ten million." For a moment she was quiet. When she turned to look at him, shock was in her eyes. "That's unbelievable, a staggering sum."

"You didn't know?" He was surprised at that.

"No. I haven't been in touch with anyone at home for a long time. You said there was another assassin and that he'd been outsourced. How good is he?"

His thumb stopped skimming along her collarbone. He knew what she was asking. Was Sid better than he was? Could Josh stop him if they met face-to-face?

He shook his head. "Like I said earlier, he's never failed. Word is he's not alone. I need to get you home where there are the resources to keep you safe."

Seconds seemed to tick by and felt more like minutes. Outside, the silence seemed to whisper of danger.

How far did her trust reach? His gaze met hers. He wanted to explain to her what she meant to him. Yet he didn't know himself. He only knew that no matter what danger they danced around, he would protect her with his life.

"It's a game for you." She frowned. "I don't mean like that, but I think you live for the challenge. That every assignment is like that for you, including this one."

"Never that, Erin." His hand covered hers. "You mean more to me than that." He lifted the palm of her hand to his lips and brushed a kiss across it. "I don't know how it happened, but I think I've fallen for you."

"Fallen?"

Her hand remained in his.

"Fallen," he repeated, surprising himself.

He kissed her then, parting her lips, her body pressing against his, the feel of her soft against his chest, the need for more was overwhelming.

More wasn't where they should be going. They had no future. He couldn't compromise her like that. He couldn't, wouldn't…

He let her go and dropped his hands.

"I'm sorry."

She shifted away from him. "Do you know that my sister, Sarah, was pregnant?"

It was a statement that seemed to come out of nowhere, and he didn't know what to say. Instead, he said nothing.

"I wasn't happy about it. The guy was a mistake, as she says. Not in the picture. She's too unsettled and she's going to be raising a child as a single parent. I should be there for her, instead…" She choked back a sob but a tear slipped from beneath her lashes.

He wiped it away with his thumb. It had been too much for her. He knew that. Most civilians would have collapsed by now. Not Erin.

She looked at him. Her eyes shimmered with unshed tears. "I'm probably an aunt now, and I may never know if it's even a boy or a girl. You know, despite all my original misgivings, I want to know that." She shook her head. "I'm sorry. I'm not usually a crier and that's all I seem to be doing."

He smiled at her, taking her hands in both of his. "She had the baby and both of them are healthy and well."

"Oh, my God." Her hand went to her mouth. "Why didn't you tell me sooner? I'm an aunt." She laughed a rather startled giggle.

"She had the baby ten days ago from what I've heard. A boy." He squeezed her hands. "She was placed under protective custody two weeks ago and we had to pull one of our female field workers in—midwife in a previous profession."

"A boy," she murmured. She looked up at him, and he could see the questions in her eyes, her doubt that it was true and that they were both safe.

"They're both fine, Erin. I promise."

"I believe you," she said. "It's just that… He'd have a name already I suppose…"

"Liam," Josh said. "The baby's name is Liam." His hand covered hers. He knew what a shock this was for her. Not having family near, with a mother who was troubled and needy, with little concern for her adult children's lives, it had made the sisters close. It had surprised him when he'd first discovered that particular piece of her life. It was not how it had been with his mother but every family was different.

Silence hung between them.

He let her lead, knowing she was overwhelmed, and sad that she had missed it all. "She's okay? They're both okay?"

"More than fine. Big baby, from what I heard." He shrugged. "No idea of weight, hair color or lack thereof, so don't ask. Sarah has been prepping for the trial. She's going to testify."

"No." She stood up. "She can't do it. I won't…" She stopped.

He took her hand and pulled her back down beside him. "It's going to be fine. We just have to get you home."

"It's been so long since home has been anything more than a word, a moving target I could never reach. At least that's how it all felt. I know it hasn't been that long but…"

Josh put an arm around her shoulder. She felt right there, leaning against him. She fit. Like they were meant to be together. But he'd known that hours ago; it was only now that he admitted it.

"I'm sorry, I shouldn't have…" she said as she pulled away and stood up.

He followed her, brought her back against his chest, the feel of her heart beating like the quiver of a small, frightened animal. Yet she was no frightened animal. She was a grown woman, courageous and one who had hours ago hit the wall of her endurance.

His lips brushed hers, the feel of them achingly soft. Her breath was warm and seductive and his tongue caressed her lips, teasing them open. He brought her body close to his, relishing the soft feel of it against him. His hand dipped down the slim waist and over the seductive curve of her hips. She fitted against him as if she'd been meant only for him. The thought brought a rush of passion and desire and his hands only wanted to strip her of the clothes that stood between them, to plunder and make her his.

He couldn't do that—she was too vulnerable. He'd be taking advantage.

She cupped his face with her hands and kissed him.

It was a kiss that removed any doubts, and he kissed

her back. He took charge, pushing her hands aside and wrapping his arms around her.

But she met him kiss for kiss, her tongue sending shivers through him as she tasted his lips, his neck. Her fingers were like pulse points of heat on his skin as she ran them under his T-shirt, flirting with his firm belly, going upward. He bent down, his lips meeting hers, his hands beginning to undo the buttons of her blouse.

"I'm stronger than you think. I survived five months on the road," she whispered, her breath hot against his neck.

"You were amazing. I couldn't help but admire what you did. The container ship, brilliant." He pushed her blouse partway off her shoulders.

She pushed his T-shirt up as her fingers roamed over his muscled chest.

"Josh?" Her hand dropped.

"Don't stop now." It was all he could think to say.

"I didn't plan to," she said in an oddly breathy voice. "I just want to rid us of this T-shirt. It's getting in the way." She took a step back and pulled an arm free of her blouse.

"You're a mind reader," he said as her blouse fell to the ground and was soon joined by his T-shirt. He cupped her breast. Her nipple pressed hard against his palm—and he was hard. She was caressing him, and it was too much. His hand closed over hers.

He unzipped her shorts, pulling them down.

"Let me," she said but instead she reached for him and within seconds there were no clothes between them.

The small room seemed too much, everything was too close—the world seemed to stop and then in a way, impossibly, heat up. She was like no other woman—he felt out of control and he didn't want that, yet he wanted it all—all of her.

He bent her backward over his arm, his lips ravaging

hers, claiming one breast and then the other. She pulled him down to the mattress where her hands also slipped down to where he held on to his control by a thread.

He pulled away from her, pinning her hands as he trailed kisses down her throat, the same way she had done to him so many minutes earlier.

He cupped her hip, running a thumb along the inside of her leg.

Where this was going—there could be nothing after. His job, his lifestyle…she abhorred risk. She'd said so.

He wanted her more than the job. It was a random thought, something that flitted through the mire of desire.

His hand held her breast, toying with her nipple as his other hand explored farther, running fingers between her legs, caressing her until she told him in a way words never could how ready she was.

"There's no turning back, Erin."

Had he said that? He wasn't one to second-guess anything and most especially sex, but with her it was different. With her he wanted it to be perfect. And it was, as she rode him to ecstasy.

And when it was all over, they lay silently side by side, but after a few minutes he leaned over and kissed her, and she ran her hands over his body and he needed no convincing that they should begin it all again.

And as the night deepened, the threats and the thought of death were liquefied in the heat of passion.

Chapter Twenty-Four

Thursday, October 15, 4:00 a.m.

She slept curled up as if in a cocoon. Her knees were pulled up to her stomach, her feet were curled around his, her plush derriere pushed against his groin and teasing him to begin it all over again.

He shifted away.

There were other things to consider despite his readiness, despite his body's driving reminder that he wanted her and he wanted her now. He'd been awake the past hour going through the events of the evening, through the details of their escape from Mulu and backward further to that afternoon. It was a procedure he followed in every assignment, covering all the bases, making sure he'd missed nothing. He'd gone back to that evening, to the plane and to Wade. There he found the inconsistency, the niggling moment of doubt that made him consider possibilities that he once would have thought implausible.

No more.

Now he suspected they'd been compromised. That was always a possibility and not a shocking one to realize. But it was the man he suspected that made him not want to believe.

He stood up. There were times when he had to follow his gut and this was one of those times. Something told him to check the status of the Georgetown airport directly with the airport authorities. He headed down to the hotel's shabby office and within ten minutes he was back, the expression on his face grave. The airport had never been closed—there was no accident, no crash. Yet, Wade had admitted on the flight that he'd personally informed Tenuk of the Georgetown Malaysia's temporary closure. There was no reason for Wade to admit that to him unless he was so secure in his lie that he could accept sole responsibility.

"Damn it," he muttered and his fist clenched as he realized what Wade had done. It had been hidden by Wade's habit of dressing more like the locals in tropical climates and wearing a long-sleeved cotton shirt despite the heat. He swore that it kept him cooler than exposed skin. He remembered what he should have noticed then, the small tattoo, covered by his sleeve. It was nothing noticeable, not to anyone else and for a while, not even to him. It had been that tidbit of information that one takes in but doesn't acknowledge until later. He should have been aware of it immediately. But there'd been too much going on.

No. He shook his head. That was leeway you gave the ordinary man. It wasn't something he gave himself.

"One day if I can ever retire, I'm getting a tattoo," Wade had said, a year ago on another beach, in another time—a different assignment. "On my wrist. Freedom. And then I'm getting the hell out. Thing of it is, I don't think that time will ever come. My retirement dreams are too pricey."

Wade had dreamed big and retirement had been a nonentity for him. He'd said many times that his ex-wives cost him too much in alimony and three kids still in college drained him of everything he made.

But somehow Wade had found the money; the tattoo proved it. He couldn't believe he'd missed that tattoo, but thinking back now, it had been inconspicuous, small and almost flesh-colored. He suspected it would be enhanced later—when Wade was truly free. But now he'd realized what he'd missed. The small bird positioned like a rocket taking off on his friend's wrist was a glaring oversight. The thought made him more than uneasy and he still wanted to deny it but what clinched it all was the check on the status of Georgetown's airport over the past few hours. It had all been a ruse.

He'd come back to bed, to check on Erin, to hold her and to think.

Tenuk.

He had repeated the information from Wade. It was his job to check. Why hadn't he?

And then there was Mike Olesk, the man who had given Erin the idea to run. Mike Olesk was the man who had told her to go to Georgetown and to the place where she had been compromised.

They were no longer safe. Wade and possibly Mike Olesk had turned. Whether there were others, no matter how many there might be, didn't matter. Not now. The only thing that mattered was that they were on their own and they had to get the hell out of here.

His hand brushed her shoulder. He lifted a strand of hair and stroked along her arm, trying to ease her from sleep to wakefulness without scaring her. She shifted but didn't wake up. Another time he would have smiled at the thought for it was another sign that she trusted him and that she felt safe.

He looked at his watch.

He had no idea how much time they had, but he suspected Wade's promised afternoon pickup was null and void. The tattoo raised all kinds of flags including an in-tuition that screamed danger. It was an intuition that he had learned not to ignore.

She turned over and blinked, looking at him with a sleepy, passion-dredged gaze.

"You have to get up, get dressed."

"What?" She sat up. She was awake in an instant, a skill he suspected she'd learned early on in her flight.

"We're getting out," he said in a throaty whisper. "We've been compromised."

"Wade?" she whispered.

He looked at her startled. "What…?"

"Women's intuition and the look on your face. You look devastated. Only a friend can do that. He was a friend, wasn't he?"

"I thought so."

"What happened?"

"No time for explanations. Except to say I think he's run into a pot of money that will make him a free man."

"The ten million?" She frowned.

"Exactly. That and a little tattoo on his wrist that says he's a free man—able to retire early." He held out his hand, lifting her off the bed. "Wade doesn't—didn't," he corrected, "have that kind of money."

She frowned. "You're sure?"

"I'm not so sure of anything right now. Except that we need to get out."

She reached down, grabbed her shorts and top.

Moonlight stripped patterns of faint light across the small room and seemed to highlight the urgency by casting her face in shadows.

"You're safe, Erin," he said, sensing her inner qualms. "I won't let anything or anyone harm you. I promise."

"Josh." She laid a hand on his arm. "I know that and

I trust you, but you've got to know that you can rely on me, too."

"Fair enough."

Fifteen minutes later they were on the path leading to the beach. The night sky was just beginning to lighten.

Damn, he thought, he would have preferred the cover of complete darkness. They'd have to move fast.

"What now?" she asked as they trekked along the hard path that led to the beach.

"Tenuk arranged a fishing boat. It's waiting to get us off this damn island before we're trapped here," Josh said, squeezing her hand. That was one problem solved. Tenuk had followed up with the Georgetown airport and discovered Wade's lie. He'd been notified by Tenuk only five minutes ago that there was a breach in security and that another Special Forces agent would be meeting them by boat to get them off the island. The conversation had made it clear that Tenuk wasn't his problem. In fact, the information Tenuk provided only confirmed what he already knew—that the leak was somewhere else. And all of it circled back to Wade. There was a hollow feeling in his gut at the thought, but it was nothing he could dwell on. He had to focus on their current situation.

He could see a figure down the beach more than sixty feet away and faint in the darkness. Beside him, Erin rubbed her elbows, her arms folded as if protecting herself.

"Get down," he hissed. "Just in case."

She sank down into the sand, and he knew that if nothing else she would feel less exposed.

The man who had met them at the airport emerged from a thicket of scrub brush maybe twenty-five feet ahead.

"Stay here," he said to Erin. "Stay down," he repeated

before he went over to the small man who appeared to be wearing the same *longyi* he had worn earlier.

"The boat is waiting," the man said in Malay. He waved his hands as he spoke.

Josh nodded, listened as he was briefed on logistics and then turned to go back and get Erin. It was time, time to get her out.

"C'mon, Erin, we've got ourselves a trip booked." He kept his voice light, trying to dispel all the fear and urgency that already had her on edge. "We're taking a boat out of here." He repeated that information as if confirming what he already knew and what he had so recently told her. Maybe in repeating the fact that they were getting out, he could keep her focused—calm. Except, he was surprised as he looked at her, to see that she was looking completely together. The earlier tears were gone, as were any questions or doubts about his motives. She was quietly moving beside him, shadowing him. He couldn't ask for more. "Do you have any motion sickness tablets?"

"Yes, but…"

"Take them. We're in a small boat on a sea known for making people ill."

She stopped and opened her pack. The leather pouch he knew had a steel cord that she told him had remained around her waist through her entire trip. She took a pill and handed him one.

He shook his head, returning it to her. "No. They make me sleepy."

"And you need your wits about you." She dropped both pills back into the container. "You need me to be alert, too, and I don't normally get sick."

They headed down the beach. The sand seemed to stretch endlessly on either side, highlighted by a half-moon that lit a strip of the beach and aided by the rapidly lightening sky. Sixty feet down the beach and another forty feet from shore, a weathered fishing boat waited. It was smaller than he'd expected, not much more than thirty feet in length. He frowned and considered the size of the ferries that plied the Andaman Sea along the Malaysian coastline. This boat was much smaller. It could be a rough ride even in a bigger boat. This one might make it a bit more arduous, but there was no choice.

In the distance he could see the gleam of red of the outboard motor and then the light slipped and the boat fell into the shadows. Jungle bracketed them to the right, screening and providing a border between the beach and whatever lay beyond.

"Move quickly," Josh said as he prodded her with his hand in the small of her back.

He'd purposely put himself between her and the jungle, because it was from there that trouble would come. His hand fingered his Glock and his gaze ran along the perimeter to where jungle briefly met sand and their waiting transport.

Waves swept onto the shore, not overly large but with enough weight to make a constant crashing sound that broke the stillness. Unfortunately it masked the sound of other things, other dangers. The boat was maybe seventy feet away now, anchored just off shore. The driver would be there to meet them in five minutes, hopefully less. At least that was what his intelligence source here had said, and it was what Tenuk had communicated to him.

He didn't like it.

They were too open. He considered heading toward the jungle, crouching there until their driver showed up. But five minutes wasn't that long and he knew the man who would be taking them in this boat. And he knew that he wouldn't be a minute less than the five minutes, they'd been told.

As those thoughts crossed his mind there was the sound of gunshot and a flash. It lit a spot in the jungle, pinpointing where the shot had been fired.

"Damn!" He hissed as a slice of pain drove through his left arm.

"Josh?" Erin's voice was barely audible.

"Get down!" He pushed her to the sand with one arm. His other arm was numb but already beginning to throb. He knew debilitating pain would happen soon, and he knew he had to power through.

The shot had come from not thirty feet to their right, from the shelter of the jungle.

Find cover.

Get out of the open.

The thoughts jammed together in the seconds that followed as he flattened her to the sand, as they crawled forward, the rough grains digging into his elbows. She was right beside him, matching him inch for inch, watching him as he tried to keep his injured arm away from the sand, from pressure—the pain so fresh it threatened to take him down.

"We're going to stand up and when we do, run straight toward the boat. Then we're going to hit the water, go under and swim the rest of the way underwater to the boat."

"You can't, Josh. You're injured. And I—"

"Run," Josh commanded a moment later.

Flashes of light, this time closer, maybe twenty feet to their right.

More gunshots.

She had a grip on his good arm, pulling him along, as he kept his back to the jungle, between her and the shooter.

Something hot and warm trailed down his arm, and his breath was coming too heavy. He was bleeding. He didn't know how bad it was, and he couldn't think about it. His head spun, he was light-headed—loss of blood, maybe shock. He couldn't let it take him down.

"Josh."

"Keep going," he hissed, squeezing her hand, freeing his arm.

"You're bleeding."

She stumbled, and he grabbed her with his good arm. He tasted blood as he bit the inside of his lip, matching the pain in his arm with something more acute—a temporary block he'd learned a long time ago, one pain, no matter how small, temporarily masking another.

A man rose from the underbrush not forty feet to their right. Heavyset, he was dressed in what looked like fatigues, with dark hair and an even darker outline of a gun.

Erin screamed and then covered her mouth.

As the man raised his gun, Josh dropped Erin's hand and raised his Glock. His hand wavered for a moment and one blast of gunfire followed another. The dark shadow on the edge of the jungle fell. And it was as if everything went still.

"I doubt he was alone," he said and he couldn't keep the pain from his voice.

"Lean on me," she said.

He gripped her shoulder with his left hand and even that was painful. He shifted his gun and for a minute the pain put him off balance. He eased up as he realized that his fingers were biting into her flesh. "I'm sorry."

"Don't be," she whispered. "Let's just get you to that boat."

He clenched his teeth. This wasn't how it was supposed to be. And again he leaned on her as pain tore through his arm and blood pooled in his palm before dropping to the sand.

"Thank goodness for the morning workouts." She laughed, a strained sound in the shifting and rapidly lifting darkness.

He let go of her shoulder and stood straight. They couldn't get to the boat and defend themselves like this. Blood streamed down his side.

"Give me your gun," she said.

"What?" Now he was sweating, and again the world seemed to spin. His hand went to the Glock. "No way. I'll be fine."

"You're in no shape to use it and if there's someone else… If he's not dead…"

A shot sounded to their right. She was flattened to the sand, he was on top of her, firing back. It was the only way to keep her safe, as uncomfortable as it might be for her, his body a shield for hers.

Silence. Seconds ticked by, a minute—the silence continued.

He rolled off her.

"You're all right?" He would have helped her up, but his damn arm was now almost useless and the other was occupied with the gun.

He could see the raw fear in her eyes and that fear was mixed with disbelief and something else: determination.

She didn't ask for the gun again. He suspected that was a moot point now. The only point that was relevant was to get to that boat. "We need to get out of here now!"

"You're bleeding." She seemed fixated on that. He supposed that was normal. Shock maybe.

"It's not that bad, Erin. It just needs a bandage and an aspirin—maybe a stitch or two. We'll have plenty of time once we're on the water."

A shot, this time to the left, and he could almost feel the heat of the bullet.

"Hell!" Josh muttered and they hit the sand again. He rolled with her, his arm around her, the gun pointing out, away from her.

Once.

Twice.

This time he was careful to keep his weight from her, but it wasn't easy and he wasn't one hundred percent successful. He knew from her stifled groan that he had crushed her into the sand. He rolled again, this time his injured arm took their combined weight and he grunted as pain shot through him. Then they were positioned flat-out on their bellies. A perfect position to take aim, and this time he needed to get their pursuer. He'd already determined that his thought of more than one was wrong. There was one and there wasn't going to be another chance. Here the jungle met the beach in a triangle, bringing the cover the sniper was enjoying closer to them. Flattened to the sand, they had a chance.

One shot.

Two.

Three.

Again, the shots were coming from ahead and slightly to their left. Now they were against the lower brush that straggled on the outer edges of the jungle as foliage met sand and came close to the ocean.

Complete cover finally.

Josh lifted up, pressing on one elbow, covering Erin as he fired back. He estimated that the sniper was less than twenty feet away. An answering volley again from the left and just behind them as their Malay fisherman joined in. He counted off as silence settled on the beach.

He rose to his knees, pulling her up with him. Blood

was streaming down his arm. The boat engine droned in the sudden quiet.

"Let's go." He pulled her to her feet.

"Oh, my God," she muttered, her hair wild and tangled, falling across her face. Her hand shook in his. "You're okay?"

"That's my line. I'm fine. Let's get moving." He pushed her in front of him, putting himself again between her and the beach. The boat was so close now, not twelve feet off shore. He plunged into the water after her. It was warm on his ankles and he wanted to ram his aching arm into it.

Instead, he pushed her ahead of him while the boat bobbed in the water.

There was silence between them, and he tossed the plan to swim for it. The boat was closer than he thought.

"An armed fisherman?" she asked with a touch of humor in her voice as she reached for the ladder.

He smiled at the effort to find humor in a situation that was outside the reality of a schoolteacher's norm. He supposed the past five months had all been out of her norm. "Malaysian Special Forces," he explained.

"Fisherman on the side." The Malay man smiled and reached a hand over the boat, helping Erin in. He then reached a hand to Josh.

"At least they didn't get your shooting arm," he said as Josh swung into the boat with a grunt.

Within seconds they were away from the beach and from the danger that had threatened their lives.

"Who were they?" she asked.

"I don't know," he replied. "I can only assume it was another bounty hunter, executioner, whatever you want to call it, sent by the Anarchists."

"Thank God we didn't have to swim underwater," she said.

"That was the least of your worries." His smile was tight as he held his bad arm.

The boat swung around and headed into the warming light of early morning. The ocean was shadowed and silent.

He grimaced as another pain shot through him and his arm throbbed. Blood seeped through his fingers.

"I need something to wrap this with. Your blouse is cotton."

"I've got one better," she replied. She opened her pouch and pulled out a roll of fabric bandage.

"Is there anything you don't keep in there?" he asked and bit his lip as he pushed the sleeve of his T-shirt higher and pain shot through him.

"Fortunately I took some first aid," she muttered. "It's bad, but looks like the bullet went straight through."

He clenched his teeth as she bound the wound, and the blood seeped slowly around the edges.

Erin finished and then held the back of her hand under her nose.

The smell of the fish, the roll of the waves—he imagined it was all getting to her.

"Feeling queasy?"

She nodded. "But I'm still voting no on anti-nausea medication."

"Don't feel shy about taking it later. This ride's rough, like I said, and we've only just begun."

"Where are we going?"

He admired the fact that it was the first time she'd asked that question. She had allowed him to take her from apparent safety into danger and with no idea where they might be going.

"We're going to Thailand. It's our only option, Erin."

Ten minutes in and Josh's arm was a dull throb. Everyone was quiet. Erin, he imagined, was immersed in her own thoughts. He had been going over the logistics of what had just happened and Bob, as he preferred to be called, was concentrating on guiding the boat in a sea that was far from placid. Even in daybreak the water was thick and dark, the waves battering against them. The throb of the engine and the slap of waves was the only sound and it was eerie.

"We're going to make it, babe."

"I know," she said with a smile that quivered. "I never doubted you."

THEY'D BEEN AT sea for over an hour. Erin wasn't sure how much more she could endure without giving in and taking something to stop her stomach from heaving. She reached over and placed a hand on Josh's good arm as if doing that would somehow settle her stomach and her nerves. His heat seemed to transfer back to her, to give her confidence. The only thing it didn't do was stop the roiling in her stomach that was a combination of fear and motion sickness. His hand covered hers, and she took a temporary breath of relief. She could make out a fishing boat farther out to sea and watched as it disappeared into the horizon.

Relief swept through Erin, and she released her grip on Josh's arm. She hadn't realized she'd been holding on so tightly, but she was still imprisoned by his hand.

"You're all right?"

"Fine," she assured him. "How's the arm?"

"Hurts like a bitch, but the bleeding slowed down." He held out his arm where no more blood had seeped through the bandage since she'd first applied the wrap. He leaned over and squeezed her hand with his good one. "You're going to be fine."

"I know." She smiled faintly back at him. And what

she knew was that if they made it safely home, it was all thanks to Josh. She couldn't think of it, of what lay behind and even what lay ahead. "You're going to be fine, too."

"Thanks to you," he said.

"The least I could do," she said and smiled. "Seeing as you wouldn't hand over the gun." She paused. "I can use it, you know."

"I never doubted," he replied. "But I appreciate your bandaging skills more."

Bob turned the boat closer to land, and she could see that he was angling toward shore. The voyage was almost over. They weren't safe but soon...

"Not much farther," Josh confirmed.

Another wave of nausea ran through her. She swallowed and turned to him. "I'll be happy once we get off this boat." He squeezed her hand and said something, she presumed in Malay, to Bob. And she was reminded of how accomplished Josh was, that he wasn't just bilingual but trilingual and possibly more, that there was much about Josh that she didn't know, that she would never know. For no matter how she looked at it, they could never be a couple. Josh was a man without home or family, who was definitely much too risky to love.

Well over an hour after they left Langkawi behind they were on land, in another country.

Thailand.

In the distance she could see a longboat, and to the right the distant speck of the boat that had brought them here. Ahead there was nothing to differentiate this strip of beach from the one they had just left. It was deserted, sheltered by jungle that acted as a backdrop.

Around them was the salty scent of ocean. The morning sun gleamed across it as the beach seemed to stretch endlessly.

"Let's get off this beach," Josh said, taking her hand and moving forward and toward a break in the jungle that had been hidden by rock and foliage. It was a small rock outcropping where the greenery fell back and sand and rock replaced it. They made their way around the cliff where the jungle fell away and open land stretched in front of them.

"Your arm?"

"Can wait. We've got a rendezvous out of here."

Overhead, there was a sound that was distant and vaguely familiar.

"Helicopter," Josh said shortly. "I notified Vern. Wade's been taken out of commission. They're extracting us."

"Extracting?"

"This way." He had her hand in a grip that suggested there was no time for questions. "It's taking us up to Trang. A city in Thailand," he answered her silent question. "Where we're taking a plane out."

"You're in no shape…"

"The Anarchists have pulled out the stops. There's no choice. Thailand is no longer any safer than Malaysia. The only place where you're safe is in custody in the States. We can control things better there. I'm in no shape to do it here."

Wind kicked up overhead as the helicopter lost altitude over the beach.

Then it was landing, wind lifting the sand, spinning it, throwing grit into their eyes. Through squinted eyes she could see the pilot, a silhouette against the glass.

It was all too surreal. Erin's throat was dry and she couldn't have spoken if she had wanted to. She was moving on autopilot, trusting that Josh would get them out. And she supposed that he trusted the shadowy figure in the helicopter and the fact that he could get them some-where safe.

Home.

Was home safe?

Was anywhere safe?

They were on board even as the questions swirled.

As they settled in their seats, the pilot reached into a canvas bag at his side and pulled out a manila envelope. "Here."

Josh took the packet, and the pilot turned around, adjusting his headset.

Erin pulled the safety strap over her shoulder as the helicopter lifted, tilting as it gained altitude. She glanced at Josh, curious as to what he had, what this meant and yet feeling too overwhelmed to ask.

"New ID," Josh said as he handed her passport.

"British," she said with a frown. "Ann Worthington? I don't…"

"Sound British? But you've acted."

She knew that what he said wasn't a question, that the research he'd obviously done would have more than likely shown that she'd taken an acting class in university; and while it wasn't a passion or even a hobby, she had acted in more than a few plays.

She nodded. "Amateur."

"And in real life you were good enough at acting to disappear, resurfacing as someone else."

She nodded again.

"So now, say as little as possible. And worse case, you've been living abroad, the accent diluted as a result."

She knew that she looked doubtful.

"It's the last time. We'll be on a secure flight home by later this morning. And the trial begins in early November," he said over the noise of the engine. "The fake ID is only an extra precaution. I doubt if you'll need it."

Her smile was one of relief as they spoke briefly and easily of other things, their conversation bracketed and secure within the noise that separated them from the pilot.

"A month." Her heart beat hard in her chest.

"And it's over. There's enough evidence with what Sarah saw."

"I hate the thought of that."

"I know." His hand covered hers. "And once she's testified…"

"I disappear," she finished for him. "But I disappear with Sarah."

"Maybe," he replied. "But if you have to disappear again, you won't be disappearing alone."

"What are you suggesting?"

His lips claimed hers and he drew her against him. "You're mine and nothing's going to change that."

"You're awfully confident."

"Confidence has gotten me out of a jam or two."

"That's what I'm afraid of, Josh," she said honestly. "What you call a jam."

The ocean sprawled an azure blue to their left, and to their right, as the helicopter tilted into a turn, the morning sun reminding them of a new day as it glared through the window. A new day where there was another land and the hope of home.

His good hand settled over hers. "Maybe I've had enough danger for one lifetime."

Chapter Twenty-Five

Wednesday, November 17

Guilty—the leader of the Anarchists was going down.

"You're safe," Josh whispered in her ear. "Sarah's safe. It's over."

"Safe?" Was there such a thing?

"Yes, safe," he repeated firmly. "And without Sarah testifying. That's the beauty of it all."

She looked around. It was hard to believe. The plain, cream-colored walls hadn't changed. The box-like apartment had been her home for a month. Outside, snow was falling lightly. The weather was colder than normal for midfall in Whitefish, Montana. This was where she'd been detained, hidden while they were stateside. It was the first time she'd seen Josh since coming home and she'd missed him more than she wanted to admit, more than she'd thought possible.

"There are no others. The Anarchists have been taken out at the knees. There's nothing you can do to them. And it turns out that one of their members turned state's evidence. They never needed Sarah."

"All of it was for nothing," she murmured.

"Except that no one knew that it would come to that."

His arm settled over her shoulders, drawing her up against him. "What Sarah saw now means nothing."

"Thank goodness," she murmured, leaning into him and all that he offered.

"No more worries."

"An understatement," she said and turned to him with a smile.

His hand covered hers. "No more running."

Her smile broadened. Just that morning, in anticipation of this very news, she'd agreed to a full-time teaching job with kindergarten children. It was halfway across the country from her sister and her new nephew, but at least Tampa was in the country. Her days of running were behind her.

"It was too bad about Wade," she murmured. "You trusted him."

"To a point. But truly, in that line of work you doubt everyone."

She noted the past tense, wondered at it for a moment and moved on.

"Even Mike." She sighed. "I can't believe that he was that far in debt or that he was able to be bribed."

"He had a gambling problem but he didn't cave in until the last minute. He swore that he thought you'd be safe by then, that you'd left Georgetown. He'd never imagined you'd still be there." He cleared his throat. "If that's any justification."

She shook her head. She'd lost contact with Mike after she'd arrived in Georgetown. That had been his last bit of advice—go deep and break contact. Now she realized that in an odd way he'd given her a head start before offering up what he knew for what money he could get. In an odd way he'd protected her before betraying her.

"I trusted him. But he wasn't a friend. As an adult I wasn't close to him. Should that make me feel any better?"

"Betrayal is betrayal. He's going to be facing a court date of his own, if that's any consolation. As for Wade, I suspect early retirement isn't in the cards for him, either. Can't say I feel sorry about that one. He had you facing an executioner for a paltry sum, not even the full reward."

"Paltry?"

"It's just money. History tells us how little that can be worth at the whim of a government—think Vietnam or Cambodia. There were times in the twentieth century when their currency meant nothing. Millionaires became paupers overnight at the whim of a corrupt government. It can happen anywhere."

"Josh." She squeezed his hand. "It's all right to feel like crap because your friend betrayed you. No need to divert with a history lesson."

"Divert?" He smiled slightly. "You're right. Wade took me out at the knees, at least for a day or two. I didn't expect that of him. But you're wrong about one thing. Like I said before, he wasn't a close friend."

"Still, like you said, betrayal is betrayal. He endangered you and would have had me killed for money. It's unbelievable." And she thought of how, for Josh, it was all about making it right. She knew without him saying it that the money had always been secondary.

"Maybe after all this we need a vacation," Josh suggested. He looked at her with a rather impish expression on his face.

"Vacation?" The thought of flying, of going anywhere after all the months of travel, of flight, was off-putting. She'd put the Canadian and British passports into safe-keeping, but she'd yet to pull out her American passport. She had no desire to go anywhere.

"I thought maybe a spa."

"Spa?" The thought of Josh going to a spa, of him enjoying the experience, was improbable. The fact that he would do it for her was, well, it was a self-sacrificing gesture.

"Something wrong with that?"

"Maybe a real trip."

He laughed, the sound deep and throaty. "Maybe we need to meet somewhere in the middle."

"Maybe," she agreed.

He reached over, pulling her to him. The strength and ease with which he did it attested to how quickly he'd healed. Stitches and a round of antibiotics had replaced her field dressing, and now there was only a scar to remind them of the bullet that was meant to kill.

"Maybe? Time alone doesn't sound romantic to you?"

"That spa you mentioned?" She grinned up at him. "I don't know."

"We'd be together." He drew an arm around her shoulder. "And while we're speaking of that, I have a surprise for you." He looked at the clock on the wall.

"A surprise?" She looked up at him just as his lips met hers, teasing them in a light flirtatious kiss, as she wrapped her arms around his neck deepening the kiss and drawing more as she met him kiss for kiss. It was he that drew away first, holding her at arm's length.

"First, the surprise," he said, his voice thick with passion. He ran a forefinger over her lower lip. "For any more kisses, I will want to take you to bed at a completely inappropriate time."

"Inappropriate?"

A knock at the door had Josh turning, his hand going to his gun—instinctively putting Erin behind him.

"Time?" Josh asked.

"Ten minutes to midnight," a male voice responded.

Erin's heart skipped a beat, both at the ritual and at the knowledge that the phrasing meant that there was another agent, a bodyguard on the other side, and what that might mean.

Josh put a hand on her shoulder. "Precautionary," he said as he went to the door and opened it. A broad, dark-haired man silently filled the doorway before nodding at Josh and stepping back.

"Sarah!" Erin breathed as a slight, young woman with an anxious expression took a step forward and then another. Her strawberry-blond hair was tied back in an understated bun, and she held a baby wrapped tightly in a pale green blanket. She was hunched almost protectively over it.

For a minute emotion and shock kept her standing, staring at her sister and the small bundle she held.

A slow smile spread over Sarah's face as she bridged the distance between them.

Erin threw her arms wide, drawing her sister into an awkward hug, conscious of the baby between them. "I can't believe you're here. That you're safe." She took a step back, her hands still on Sarah's shoulders.

Tears filled Sarah's eyes. "Thanks to you. I can't thank you enough. Erin…" She choked on the words. "You could have died. I was so scared."

"But I didn't," Erin said firmly.

Sarah shook her head. "I prayed every night for you, between that and the fact that you're the smartest person I know and the best, I knew you had to make it."

"Sarah…" Erin felt her face flush at the compliments and with the joy of seeing her sister after so many months.

"And it's finally over." Sarah shifted the bundle in her arms and looked back at the man who hovered in the doorway. "Almost."

"My nephew?" Erin breathed and wiped her eyes with the back of her hand.

"Liam," Sarah said and smiled as she pulled the blanket back.

"The name suits him," Erin said as she looked down at the baby with the dusting of reddish-blond hair whose face furrowed while he continued to sleep.

"It was Grandfather's."

"I know," Erin replied, for the first time contemplating the significance of that name and feeling surprise that Sarah had cared enough about their ancestry to use it. She suspected that the past few months had changed many things for Sarah and that with the baby there were more changes to come. She smiled as Liam's tiny hand grabbed her pinky. His eyes opened briefly and met hers as if acknowledging her before they closed again. "I'm an aunt," she said and she knew in that moment that she was hooked. "And I'll spoil you rotten," she whispered to the now sleeping baby. "Promise."

It was two hours later, and Sarah had gone back to the hotel with the FBI agent who would shadow her until sentencing was complete. Josh had confirmed that would be a few days from now. They sat together on the stiff little couch that Erin had good-naturedly complained about on more than one occasion.

"I won't miss this place," she said softly.

"You'll love Tampa," he promised.

She looked at him and laughed. "But not the RV." But she wasn't moving to the RV. She had her own place for now, a job, a soon anticipated reunion with her cat, Edgar, and a life that she knew would include him.

"I love you, babe," he said, his voice deep with promise.

She leaned her head against his shoulder. "You're still too risky to love," she said in a flirtatious whisper.

"Maybe not." Outside, the streetlights winked on. "I suspect I'm too risky *not* to love."

Her lips met his in a kiss that was hot and yearning and spoke to a future that lay wide and open in front of them.

* * * * *

INTRIGUE

Available February 16, 2016

#1623 NAVY SEAL SURVIVAL
SEAL of My Own • by Elle James
Navy SEAL Duff Calloway's vacation turns into a dangerous mission when he meets Natalie Layne. She is in Honduras to rescue her sister from human traffickers—not to fall in love with a sexy SEAL.

#1624 STRANGER IN COLD CREEK
The Gates: Most Wanted • by Paula Graves
Agent John Blake is hiding in Cold Creek to recuperate from gunshot wounds. He never expected to thwart an attempt on Miranda Duncan's life—or to find himself falling hard for the no-nonsense deputy.

#1625 GUNNING FOR THE GROOM
Colby Agency: Family Secrets • by Debra Webb & Regan Black
PI Aidan Abbot is undercover as Frankie Leone's fiancé to clear her father's name. But the closer he gets to the truth, the more Aidan wants to protect the woman he was never supposed to fall for.

#1626 SHOTGUN JUSTICE
Texas Rangers: Elite Troop • by Angi Morgan
When a serial killer targets Deputy Avery Travis, it is up to Texas Ranger Jesse Ryder to protect her. But he'll discover that falling for his best friend's little sister is almost as dangerous as the killer stalking them.

#1627 TEXAS HUNT
Mason Ridge • by Barb Han
The man who once traumatized Lisa Moore is back—and he's deadly. Lisa turns to her childhood friend, Ryan Hunt, who risks his life and heart to help. But can Lisa ever truly escape her past?

#1628 PRIVATE BODYGUARD
Orion Security • by Tyler Anne Snell
Bodyguard Oliver Quinn can't deny his history with his new client, PI Darling Smith. But keeping her safe from a killer comes before exploring their lingering feelings.

REQUEST YOUR FREE BOOKS!
2 FREE NOVELS PLUS 2 FREE GIFTS!

HARLEQUIN®

INTRIGUE

BREATHTAKING ROMANTIC SUSPENSE

YES! Please send me 2 FREE Harlequin® Intrigue novels and my 2 FREE gifts (gifts are worth about $10). After receiving them, if I don't wish to receive any more books, I can return the shipping statement marked "cancel." If I don't cancel, I will receive 6 brand-new novels every month and be billed just $4.74 per book in the U.S. or $5.49 per book in Canada. That's a savings of at least 12% off the cover price! It's quite a bargain! Shipping and handling is just 50¢ per book in the U.S. and 75¢ per book in Canada.* I understand that accepting the 2 free books and gifts places me under no obligation to buy anything. I can always return a shipment and cancel at any time. Even if I never buy another book, the two free books and gifts are mine to keep forever.

182/382 HDN GH3D

Name	(PLEASE PRINT)	
Address		Apt. #
City	State/Prov.	Zip/Postal Code

Signature (if under 18, a parent or guardian must sign)

Mail to the **Reader Service:**
IN U.S.A.: P.O. Box 1867, Buffalo, NY 14240-1867
IN CANADA: P.O. Box 609, Fort Erie, Ontario L2A 5X3
**Are you a subscriber to Harlequin® Intrigue books
and want to receive the larger-print edition?
Call 1-800-873-8635 or visit www.ReaderService.com.**

* Terms and prices subject to change without notice. Prices do not include applicable taxes. Sales tax applicable in N.Y. Canadian residents will be charged applicable taxes. Offer not valid in Quebec. This offer is limited to one order per household. Not valid for current subscribers to Harlequin Intrigue books. All orders subject to credit approval. Credit or debit balances in a customer's account(s) may be offset by any other outstanding balance owed by or to the customer. Please allow 4 to 6 weeks for delivery. Offer available while quantities last.

Your Privacy—The Reader Service is committed to protecting your privacy. Our Privacy Policy is available online at www.ReaderService.com or upon request from the Reader Service.

We make a portion of our mailing list available to reputable third parties that offer products we believe may interest you. If you prefer that we not exchange your name with third parties, or if you wish to clarify or modify your communication preferences, please visit us at www.ReaderService.com/consumerschoice or write to us at Reader Service Preference Service, P.O. Box 9062, Buffalo, NY 14240-9062. Include your complete name and address.

HI15

Setting herself up as bait is the only way for
Natalie to find her abducted sister. But all her
training can't prepare her for the irresistible stranger
she must trust with her life.

He looked up, hoping to see Natalie at the surface, thirty feet above. She wasn't there. His heart racing, Duff hurried through the rocks. Where the hell was she?

Movement ahead made him kick harder. As he neared a large boulder, he saw fins kicking and flailing. The smooth, pale legs attached could be none other than Natalie's.

When he was close enough he could see that a man had hold of her around the neck and was feeding her a regulator. He had her arms wrapped in what appeared to be weight belts, her wrists secured behind her.

Anger spiked, sending a surge of adrenaline through Duff. He raced for the attacker, holding his knife in front of him. He'd kill the bastard if he hurt one hair on Natalie's head.

Natalie's attacker must have seen Duff. He shoved Natalie toward him and kicked away from them.

Duff grabbed her from behind and held her against him. She fought, twisting her body in a frantic attempt to get free.

Finally, Duff spun her to face him, pulled the regulator from his mouth and shoved it toward hers.

She stopped struggling and opened her mouth, accepted the regulator, blew out the water and sucked in a deep breath.

Duff turned her, slipped his knife between her wrists and sliced through the heavy weaving of the weight belt material, taking several passes before he freed her hands.

When she was free, she grabbed hold of his BCD and anchored herself with him. Natalie took another deep breath and handed the regulator to him.

They buddy-breathed for a couple more minutes until she was once again calm.

A shadow floated over them, indicating the location of the boat. One by one, they surfaced and waited their turn to climb aboard the boat.

Duff surfaced a second before Natalie.

When she came up, she spit her regulator out of her mouth and gulped in fresh air. She glared across at him. "Why the hell did you do that?"

He frowned. "What do you mean? I saved your life."

"I wasn't dying."

Find out what happens next in
NAVY SEAL SURVIVAL
by New York Times *bestselling author Elle James*

Available March 2016 wherever
Harlequin books and ebooks are sold.

www.Harlequin.com